Library of Congress Cataloging-in-Publication Data available

ISBN 978-1-338-80342-6

10 9 8 7 6 5 4 3 2 1   22 23 24 25 26

Printed in the U.S.A.   37

First edition, October 2022

Book design by Stephanie Yang

The Glass Witch

LINDSAY PUCKETT

Scholastic Press / New York

To Mamaw

In every page
Every line
Every word

Evil devours.
You've nowhere to flee.
When the Goode witch numbers
err over three.

THREE HOURS UNTIL ABANDONMENT

The problem with revenge is the good kind costs more than $3.67.

Coins jingle in my hand as I peruse each greasy aisle of the gas station, hunting for the perfect poison. I pass a spit of bloated hot dogs marked $3.99 each, grimace at a browning fruit tray for $7.50, and sidestep a mountain of five-dollar nachos with cheese so artificial, it gives off a faint radioactive glow.

And then I find it. Nestled between a six-pack of fizzy orange sodas and a crumbling sausage-and-cheese biscuit, it lurks. Waiting.

The crème de la crème of comeuppance. The reigning rajah of retribution. The Baked Alaska of just deserts.

My friends and—more importantly—*enemies*, I give you: gas station sushi.

I peek down at the money in my palm and my stomach sinks. Nowhere near the $10.99 price tag.

Squeezing my eyes and fist shut, I wish really, *really* hard for more cash to appear. In fact, I do more than wish. I find the cherry pit of my heart and, with an imaginary knife, crack it open. My powers are always weaker outside Cranberry Hollow, but there's still a tug and a warmth like sunshine that glides over my skin. My palm tingles and, hopeful, I slide open an eye.

The same measly three bills and six coins glare up at me. But, like, *literally* glare. Somehow, I've animated the presidents. Washington primps his bushy wig, Lincoln picks his nose, and there's a mocking twinkle in Jefferson's eye I don't like. Almost as if he knows I failed. Again.

I stick out my tongue and shove him, and the other dead guys, back into my pocket. The illusion will fade soon enough. It always does.

Two minutes later, feeling more defeated than ever, I slap a jumbo bag of Skittles on the checkout counter, startling the elderly cashier. He clutches the newspaper to his heart—*The Daily Cranberry*—and under the crumpled print I can just make out the headline.

Locals Prepare for Cranberry Hollow's Un-BOO-lievable Annual Halloween Events!

My insides wriggle like an overfilled Jell-O mold.

"Oh—you scared me!" the cashier says, rubbing his chest. He's got gray hair, wrinkles, and a large gap between his front teeth. A name badge on his shirt reads WE'VE GOT GAS MANAGER: HOWELL.

"Sorry," I say. And I truly mean it. I may be out for revenge, but I'm not trying to give an old man a heart attack before I'm even unpacked. That's, like, *major* villain vibes. I'm going for more of a henchman level today.

Howell grabs the pack of Skittles and runs it past the scanner. "Ah, it's all right. My hearing isn't what it used to be. Say, that's an interesting fellow," he says, nodding to the chef's face ironed on my sweatshirt, beet red and mouth open in a silent roar. He squints and reads the type. "'Are—you—an—idiot—sandwich?' My!"

I tug at the fabric, uncomfortable. I hate when people look at my body, even if it's just to read the graphics. "It's Gordon Ramsay. He's my favorite chef."

Howell gums his lip in obvious disapproval, but then his eyes travel up to my face and go wide. "Hey, you look familiar. You wouldn't be related to—"

"Bee Goode. Yeah, she's my grandma."

According to Grandma, all Goode women look alike. *Wide cheeks, wide hips, wide smiles*, she'd say with a wink, then shove an oatmeal cookie, fresh from the oven, in my mouth. I don't know about smiles—we don't do much of that—but our cheeks and hips are wide as ever.

Howell's grin pulls at his wrinkles. "Adelaide Goode! You've grown since the last time you were in town! Your mother in for a visit too? I'm sure they'd love to have her as a guest judge for the pageant tonight. The original Miss Preteen Scary Cranberry herself."

My hands knot in my sweatshirt. "She's just dropping me off. She has a plane to catch at three."

"So soon? You two haven't been for a visit in what? Five years?"

I push my glasses up my nose and shrug, trying to radiate big I-don't-care energy. "She's got a new job in Seattle. I'm staying with Grandma until she gets back."

"Oh. Now that you mention it, I think I remember something your grandma said about one of her daughters taking a traveling nurse job."

"That's her."

Howell hands me the Skittles. "Go on and take these. On the house."

A grin tugs at my lips. "Thanks."

"Anything for Bee's granddaughter." His face wiggles into a toothy, sympathetic smile. "Good old Bee Goode. She takes in strays of all kinds, doesn't she?"

My stomach deflates like an underwhipped meringue. Grumbling, I pull up my hood, jam the candy in my pocket, and head out the door.

Right next to the rickety self-serve gas pump sits Legs. And by Legs I mean my mom's forest-green clunker of a station wagon and honorary first child. Mom really christened him Last Legs, which is probably because he breaks down constantly, although he doesn't have legs at all. I guess it's supposed to be "ironic funny."

Anyway, he's the same car she drove out of Cranberry Hollow with me in her belly twelve years ago. *He's the only man that's never let me down*, Mom always said. Although she quit saying that when I got old enough to ask questions about my dad. None of which ever got answers.

I'm a pretty understanding person—villainy aside—but in the realm of normal mother-daughter relationships, keeping secrets is *not cool*. Especially when it's the one secret I'd really like the answer to.

I yank open the sticky handle and flop on the carpet seats, slamming the door shut a little too hard behind me. My glasses fog as the heater sputters, blowing the smell of melted lipstick and cheap air fresheners up my nose. Mom sits behind the wheel, applying a thick coat of lipstick—unmelted—in the pull-down mirror.

Mom looks like me but better. Her hair is red and curly, her nails buffed and polished, and her clothes bright and fashionable. But it's not her hair or clothes that make her pretty. It's how she *defies* them. Like "Yes, I'm fat, but I'm also beautiful and don't need to hide behind spandex or manicures to be allowed to exist." With that confidence, it's no wonder she won the Miss Preteen Scary Cranberry title.

I glare down at my muddy sneakers and blow frizzy orange hair out of my eyes.

"What'd you end up getting?" Mom asks. She works the magenta lipstick—Very Berry Delight—between her lips and pops it with a wet plunging sound. The noise is so dismissive, so infuriating, it boils the feelings I've been simmering all week red hot.

Here's the thing. I know she gave me candy money to bait me

6

into a better mood about the whole "staying with Grandma thing." But the truth is, ditching me while she flits off to work her dream job in her dream city feels a whole lot like the plot in one of those sad dog movies. The ones they play on planes that no one wants to watch, but you end up watching anyway because there's nothing else to do, and the next thing you know, Fido's owners leave him and you're blubbering on the way to Disney World.

For reference—I'm the abandoned dog in this situation.

And the worst part is, I know there's a small part of Mom that's excited about dumping me. Three months kid free. She can do everything she missed out on when she became a teen mom. She could live her life free of the burden of *me*. Of how I tore the family apart.

Of how I'm cursed.

I rip open the pack of candy and pour a few pieces straight into my mouth.

"Skittles, yum," Mom says. "Can I have one?"

I glare at her. Her smile is so big, so placating. It hurts my heart.

I bet this is how those owners looked at their dog before ditching him at the pound.

I shrug and pour a handful into my palm. Inspecting the colors,

I delicately place each one back in the bag until only one is left, bleeding sticky dye on my skin. I offer it to her.

Orange. Her least favorite.

Mom's cheery demeanor slips. Her nostrils flare and her lips press into a thin line. "Really, Adelaide?"

I raise an eyebrow and hoist my hand higher. She glares back but eventually sighs. With an exhausted wave of her hand, the Skittle floats out of my palm and into her open mouth. Power tugs from my skin, but it's so small Mom probably doesn't notice she tapped into my source. That can happen when you're close to a relative.

A low current of power runs through all witches' veins—enough for small tasks like levitating Skittles into your mouth or hoisting the suitcase of an unwanted daughter into the back of a legless station wagon—but bigger enchantments require more. Spells. Potions. *Kindred*.

To the shock of absolutely no one—my Kindred is weak. And for a bit of background, Goode witches aren't *supposed* to be weak. Historically, we were the strongest witches in all thirteen colonies. Just my luck.

Mother-daughter Kindred is supposed to be the easiest kind, since I lived inside her for a while and she's my oldest family. I always thought it's so hard for us because she never really wanted me to begin with, and the ancestors can tell. And now that I'm being "abandoned at the pound," things are a little worse.

The truth stings like a bee, but I've learned that if I have a stinger too, it's not so bad. I close my eyes and pretend my body is a tornado of malicious, buzzing hornets swirling under my skin. Because anger I can handle.

Mom rolls her eyes and knocks the car in gear. With a jolt and a huff, Legs rumbles out of the gas station. I stare moodily out the window, rolling a grape candy on my tongue, as trees blur by.

"I brought you something," Mom says flatly, floating her purse up from the back seat. "I was hoping to give it to you when you were being less bratty, but I guess that's not happening."

She plops the leather bag in my lap a little harder than neces-sary. I shoot her what I hope is an adequate *excuse me* face, but I slide the zipper open anyway.

Even lying on a pile of crumpled receipts, the delicate purple and turquoise petals flutter around the wooden circlet like butterfly wings. Crystal buds center each daisy, catching the afternoon sun and showering the car with orbs of light.

The crown Mom wore the night she won the Miss Preteen Scary Cranberry costume pageant.

Angry as I am, I can't help but run a finger over the velvety flowers. I know the story well—it's basically legend. Grandma and Aunt Jodie had stayed up all night before the pageant gluing, sewing, and bedazzling Mom into the finest fairy princess Cranberry Hollow had ever seen. People say she shone like the night sky. No, like, literally. Skin and hair coated in a thousand tiny crystals, she outshone the competition and won the crown.

Despite everything, warmth spreads in my belly. I can't believe she's letting me have this. I spread a protective hand over the flowers to keep the bumpy ride from snapping them.

"I thought you could wear it for the costume contest. Of course, you don't have to be anything scary—I was a fairy." I roll my eyes. Like I don't know. "But Jodie's great with crafts, and I'm sure she can make it fit whatever you want."

The warmth evaporates.

Here's a list of things I'd rather do than walk out on a pageant stage:

1. Eat stewed peas
2. Puke up the stewed peas and eat them again
3. Be cursed to eat and puke stewed peas for all eternity, without the reprieve of death

I pop another candy in my mouth and crunch hard.

"You should do the pageant, Addie. It's a great way to make friends. Plus, it'll make the time go faster."

My bees buzz, and I shove the crown in my hoodie pocket. Sequins snap off and sprinkle my lap. "Fat girls don't win pageants. Not even stupid Halloween ones."

"Who told you that?"

"Mom, I'm twelve. I go to school. I watch TV." I cross my arms and settle deep in my seat. "Everyone knows that."

It's quiet for a moment, then Mom's breath comes out in a long stream. "It's not always fair for us curvy girls, but I won when I was your age. And I was bigger than you."

"Yeah, well, that was the nineties."

"Right, *the nineties*. When the trend was to look like Mary-Kate and Ashley, and I *still* went home with a crown."

My brow lifts. "Who's Mary Kadenashley?"

Mom mumbles something that sounds like *Jesus, take the wheel.* Her eyes flit from the road to me, then something changes in her face. Softens. "You know I'm doing this for us, right?"

I don't say anything. Just offer her another orange Skittle.

Mom growls, and I stare back out the window. The trees are thicker here, with puffs of orange and yellow leaves swaying in the breeze. Most people think they're pretty, but I'm not fooled. Changing leaf color means cellular *death*. I learned that in fifth-grade science, thank you very much. And really, I'm not one for poetics, but driving into a forest of death can't be a good sign for this "new start."

Around the next bend, a wooden sign appears, falsely cheery for the dour mood.

WELCOME TO CRANBERRY HOLLOW!

Five years. That's how long it's been since I've seen that sign. Since Aunt Jodie got to glare at me. Since Mom and Grandma got in their last shouting match over nothing. Since I got to feel—

Legs clunks past the sign and something *moves* over me. It dribbles like a hot shower, sending tingles over my skin and fingers down my spine. The sensation is so strong, so wonderful, even my bees melt into a pool of honey. The cherry pit of my heart throbs. It's delicious and soft and sweet as confetti cake batter, something I can only encounter in Cranberry Hollow.

It's the feel of wild magic.

2

THREE HOURS UNTIL ABANDONMENT

Cranberry Hollow. Known for its quiet neighborhoods, insignificant historical sites, and an obscene amount of cranberry farms. On Main Street you can buy cranberry sauces, breads, and jams by the dozen. If you're feeling a bit more experimental, pop down to the Dig-In Diner for the local specialty Cranberry Carbonara or the infamous Cran-Fish Gravy.

"The cranberries are so good, they're almost magical," the *New England Inquisitor* posted last summer. A "homegrown staple in a homegrown community."

I've always hated cranberries.

The town's nice though, especially around Halloween. The locals turn up every year with decorations, festivals, and an unhealthy obsession with witches. Seriously. The visitor count at the Cranberry Hollow Witch Museum skyrockets, and Grandma's potion shop, the Goode Witch, sees a huge spike in crystal and incense sales (all nonmagic and safe—she keeps the real stuff in the back).

There's even a witch-burning dramatization in the town square. I mean, sure, the nearest witch trial happened nine counties over, but the historical re-creation makes the locals *feel* like they were really there, a part of some grand piece of American history.

I get not wanting to forget the important stuff, but there are some things people just don't want to think about. Burning women, for instance.

For me, it's that I'm the reason Aunt Jodie and Mom don't speak anymore. Or the fact that Grandma and Mom never really look each other in the eye.

We pull onto Grandma's street and the bees re-form under my skin, sharpening their stingers on my bones. Queasy, I reach in the back seat for my single solace in this poop-shack of a situation— my proverbial comfort blankie, if you will. Macarons. More specifically, my Hopefully First Place Submission to the Festival Bake-Off macarons. The one competition I have a shot at winning.

I lift the tub and inspect my cookies through the foggy plastic.

Dyed the perfect shade of Granny Smith, the apple cookies sandwich a slathering of homemade caramel cream sauce. Whipped icing dollops make the eyes, and a line of candy corn smooshed between the two cookies forms a vicious, fanged grin. Last, but not least—a pinch of sea salt dusts their tops to bring out the sweet flavors.

Just being close to meringue and icing uncoils the knot in my chest.

Mom nudges me with her phone, one hand still on the wheel. "Call Grandma for me."

"Again?"

"We need to make sure Jodie left."

"I called like an hour ago. She's gone."

"Better safe than sorry."

The rhyme, passed down generation to generation, slithers through my ears like a viper. The way it always does whenever we talk about the Goode Curse.

> *Evil devours.*
> *You've nowhere to flee.*
> *When the Goode witch numbers*
> *err over three.*

I shake off chills, then remember I'm supposed to be channeling henchman-villain energy. My eyes cut to Mom in what I think is a pretty spectacular side-eye. The call probably has more to do with her not wanting to see Aunt Jodie than the jinx, but I thumb Grandma's number in anyway. "Wouldn't we know if she wasn't gone? If it . . . activated?"

"I don't know. It's never been activated."

I put the phone to my ear. It rings five times before I hand it back. "Line's busy."

Mom does another world-class eye roll. Seriously, she could win the Olympic division if there was such a thing. "Figures."

Grandma's driveway is almost a mile long, deeper in the woods than most, and potted from recent rain. After much clunking and sputtering on Legs's part, we finally roll into a sunny clearing. A wooden sign with two long ears poking out of its top sticks out of the wet ground. GOODE RABBIT SANCTUARY, it reads.

A two-story cottage perches behind it, looking boringly average with its paint-peeled shutters and missing thatch work in the roof. Well—except for the magical purple smoke billowing from the chimney in the shape of rabbits and squirrels and unicorns dancing the cancan. That part is a little less boring.

Of course, only us witches can see it. If a normal human looked at the smoke, their eyes and brains would go all fuzzy, like someone with an eraser clearing a chalkboard. In fact, the only way they can see magic is if a witch *shows* them, on purpose or not. The rules are kind of murky, but basically once a human notices, they don't stop noticing. Which is why we have to be careful. Just ask any of the Salem witches.

Legs puffs to a stop, and Mom kills the engine. She fumbles with her purse, acting like she's looking for something inside. Maybe her courage. Or patience. Or another tube of Very Berry Delight. Either way, she's obviously putting off the inevitable. I sigh loudly so she knows I'm still annoyed and scramble out toward the trunk.

Inside, my suitcase is nestled between a spare tire and a trash bag of old clothes for charity Mom keeps forgetting to drop off. I brush it clean, then squint at the handle.

Magic pulses around me. I try to catch it, hold it in a jar like fireflies. A spark kindles in my chest and I heave with my mind. To my delight, the suitcase levitates a few inches from the trunk floor.

Then the fireflies flood through my fingers and the suitcase crashes down. I grumble, grab the handle, and manually tug it free.

Mom finally emerges from the wagon with my macarons. She notices me struggling and magics my luggage out of my arms and up the porch steps with a flick of her finger. As long as at least one Goode witch makes her home in Cranberry Hollow, magic runs thick in the air here. Not even a pinch of Kindred pulls from my body. Of course, the magic works for *her*. *I'm* still a dud.

My disappointment must show on my face, because Mom ruffles my hair. "Just be patient. You're a Goode. Your magic will figure itself out soon enough."

I rip away from her touch and smooth my curls flat. "Don't hold your breath."

But Mom doesn't hear me. She's staring up the walkway, a nervous tic in her fingers. I follow her gaze. Ahead, lazy bees pepper the lawn under the watchful eye of bunny sculptures keeping sentinel around the porch. As if sensing our magic, they wiggle their ceramic noses and cock their ears in our direction.

Someone who was less of a henchman might admit the bunny home security charm was cute, that it took the smallest edge off their anxiety, or even that they had to work pretty hard not to bend down and scratch one of their floppy ears.

I pity those weak henchmen.

"Come on," I mumble, and pull Mom by her elbow.

We trudge past the bunnies and stop before a yellow wooden door. A sign in the shape of a rabbit head is tacked in the middle.

WELCOME TO OUR WARREN!

"Ready?" she says, more to herself than me. She looks like she might be sick, or worse—drop my macarons. I grab them from her and set them on a wicker rocking chair. Then I knock.

Sounds bustle, a latch is pulled, and the door opens, wafting out the scent of gooey oatmeal cookies and straw. Of Grandma.

Wide hips, wide eyes, wide smiles.

Well, two out of three isn't bad.

Grandma stands in the doorway looking just like Mom and me but under a messy white bun with bits of hay sticking out of it. The Goode Nose, as Mom calls it—long, thin, and freckled—is perched on her lined face. Of course, I inherited one that's squat and fleshy, with nostrils so bubbled they look bee-stung. Even my *nose* can't get the Goode thing down.

All my memories of Grandma include a phone perpetually glued to her ear as she worked on some job or organized a charity event of some sort. This time is no different.

"Hold on, Carmella, I'll have to call you back. My granddaughter just arrived. No—I'm sure I've mentioned her to you before. Yes, I'll have the blueprints to you by three."

A very flustered Carmella still squawks as Grandma hangs up. Then her smile goes wide.

"Adelaide," she says, and pulls me into a warm, squishy hug. There's really nothing like a grandma hug. It's like the moment a grandchild is born, a wrinkly old fairy flies down from the heavens and says, *Congratulations! You are officially a grandparent! Here is a manual that explains the secret art of hug-giving.*

In this moment, it really feels like she wants me here.

And then, her eyes find Mom and her arms go stiff. She lets me go.

I don't actually know the specifics, but all the family pictures before my birth were of Mom, Aunt Jodie, and Grandma, arms around one another and laughing at some untold joke. Happy. Whole.

There are no post-me pictures.

"Candice. You look well."

Mom clears her throat. "We called. You didn't answer."

"I did the first time. I'm judging the bake-off at the Halloween festival and am rather busy. I've been on the phone with the mayor all morning."

We stand on the threshold for a moment, no one really looking at one another. Then Grandma plasters on a smile. "Well, come in! Come in! I've got your mom's old room ready for you, Adelaide."

With a snap of her fingers, my suitcase and Tupperware spring to life, floating in the air behind Grandma as she moves into the house. I try to catch Mom's eye, but she doesn't look at me. We follow Grandma inside.

The cottage is just how I remember it—bright and cluttered with old-lady stuff. Knitting yarn and pill bottles and fancy china you can only use if the queen visits or something. But mostly, it's cluttered with rabbits.

As soon as I'm over the threshold, a horde of multicolored bunnies sprint over to vigorously sniff my feet.

"Stephanie, that's enough of that!" Grandma chides, detangling a tiny, rambunctious Lionhead out of my shoelaces. "You've already eaten through two pairs of shoes this week. Oh, and watch out for Puddles, dear. He gets a little too excited around guests."

I lift my foot just in time to miss the—well—puddle as the floppy-eared Mini Lop twitches his nose in an apologetic grin.

We shuffle through the house, careful not to step on a black-and-white Dutch in his makeshift wheelchair or the trio of long-haired

Angoras munching on cilantro. As we pass the kitchen, a steaming tea set zooms to a stop in front of me, splashing water everywhere and flashing an array of colorful tea packets for me to choose from. I point to the purple chamomile one, and the packet bows, then rips in half and dumps the tea bag in the cup. Overhead, a cuckoo clock chimes the hour, and little bunnies and birds spring from their hutches and sing, "*Welcome back, Adelaide!*"

I can't help it—I crack a smile and wave at them. I just really, really love magic.

In the sitting room, every flat surface groans under the weight of bake-off submission boxes and tins. Sniffing rabbits circle a particularly low-sagging table like sharks around a boat, but Grandma shoos them away and clears a seat for Mom. She settles awkwardly into the squishy armchair, the tea set floating down beside her. Unfortunately for me, the only other spot is the couch, which is occupied by a solid-white bunny. It doesn't move but watches us curiously. I walk up to it and run my fingers over its fluffy ears. It does the weird little purr thing rabbits do—grinding its teeth in contentment, eyes closed. It isn't in a wheelchair, has all its limbs, and doesn't look sick.

I frown. "Who's this one?"

Grandma walks over and pats the rabbit's head. "Sweet Rosie. She's been here the longest. Passed from shelter to shelter and no one would adopt her."

"Why not?"

Rosie cocks her head at the sound of my voice. That's when I see *why*. Two ruby eyes blink up at me.

Another misfit. Abandoned. Like me.

Grandma bends down and plants a kiss on Rosie's head. "People don't like the red eyes. But I think they are the most beautiful shade of rose, don't you?"

I nod, and Rosie gets up to sniff my hand. She licks the Skittles dye off my fingers, and I laugh.

Then the doorbell rings.

"Just a minute!" Grandma calls as she bustles from the room.

Voices echo down the hall as two people emerge. One is an older man with white hair, brown skin, and kind eyes. The other is a girl my age holding a tray. Her socks and nail polish match her hijab—sky blue—and her dress is neatly ironed and covered in sparkly sequins. I can tell she's the kind of girl whose lips form a perfect heart when she smiles. When her gaze meets mine, she grins.

Yep. Perfect heart.

Rosie jumps off the couch and runs to lick the girl's ankles. Grandma follows behind them, a bushel of wildflowers in her hands. She gestures to us. "Hakeem, Fatima—this is my daughter Candice and my granddaughter, Adelaide."

I smile shyly at Fatima as Hakeem takes Mom's hand.

"Candice," he says. "Bee's told me so much about you. And your daughter, of course." His eyes travel to mine, and he shakes my hand next. He has a big toothy grin and a warm voice that's sweet and slow like molasses. It makes me feel almost the same as Grandma's hugs do. "It's wonderful to put faces to the names. And what beautiful faces they are. It must run in the family."

Everyone does that polite-adult-laugh thing and touches a hand to their chests. *Grown-ups.*

"What nice flowers," Mom says.

A slight blush rises on Grandma's cheeks as she puts them in a jar.

"Our front yard is covered with them," Hakeem says. "Last spring, I had the worst time with my garden, but then Bee came over with some new fertilizer, and voilà! I had more tomatoes and peppers than ever before." He glances back at Grandma, eyes as gooey as freshly baked fudge. "I always bring her a little of her handiwork."

Beside her, the flowers begin to change colors wildly, dancing on their stalks. Grandma quickly elbows them behind a large seven-layer cake. "Have you met Hakeem before? He lives in the house down the road. He retired about a year ago, so he comes over a lot to help out."

"We like to visit the bunnies," Fatima adds, bending down to scratch Rosie's ears. Rosie nibbles happily on the end of her shoelace.

"Yes, the bunnies," Mom says, eyes darting between Hakeem and Grandma.

I almost crack a smile because, I mean, *come on*—old-people love? Adorable. But I'm on a quest for vengeance, so I just glare at Mom instead.

"Adelaide, you remember Fatima, don't you?" Grandma asks.

"I don't think so." I think back to the last time I was here.

"You guys had a blast playing together at the Halloween festival one year," Grandma says, laughing.

A memory flashes. A girl drooling around fake plastic fangs chases me through the Halloween festival screaming spitally,

Shtay shtill sho I can drain you of blood and rip bonesh from your flesh and other vital organsh!

I eye her sparkles. This can't be the same girl. "No, sorry."

But Grandma's distracted. She glances down at the tray in Fatima's hands. "What's this, my dear?"

"My cupcakes for the bake-off!" She tilts the pan for a better view, and Grandma squawks.

Bloody icing oozes from the chocolate cakes in streams, decorative eyeballs swim in lumps of green gelatin, and something that might be chopped nuts impales the foils like broken teeth. In contrast, cute pastel flower sprinkles dust each top.

It *is* her.

I glance from the gory cupcakes to this glittery, girly Fatima and back again.

Another misfit. And if Rosie likes her, then I do too.

The Three Misfiteers.

"My! Well—those are just—" Grandma blinks rapidly, trying to form a smile. "You certainly put a lot of work into those. I'll just—um—put them over here with the others."

Grandma takes the tray from her as Hakeem chuckles into his coat collar.

"I'm entering the bake-off too," I say.

Fatima's eyes light up, flambé style. "Really?! Can I see what you made?"

"Sure." I turn to the table, but my Tupperware isn't there.

"I think Grandma might have put it in your room with the rest of your things," Mom says.

Her words make the bees growl in my stomach. "Oh, you mean *your* room? You know, where you should be staying with me instead of abandoning your only—"

"Adelaide!" Grandma and Mom scold in unison. They give nervous smiles to Hakeem, who is suddenly very interested in his cuticles.

I take a deep breath and stuff my anger down in my pocket. I'll pay for that one later.

Turning to Fatima, I ask, "Wanna come upstairs?"

She looks up at Hakeem, unbothered by the tension. "Can I, Nana?"

"Of course, meri gudiya."

The heart appears on her mouth again, fang free. Surprisingly, I find myself grinning back. I can already tell she's one of those people that make you feel less grumpy. And ancestors know I need some of that in my life.

We take off for the stairs, two at a time, hopping over snoozing bunnies and baskets of laundry. Portraits of past Goodes line the walls in crooked frames—some in color photography, a few in black and white, while others are oil paintings of stern women in bonnets and brooches. Those are few and far between though, since most of the early Goodes were killed off by hunters.

And if what Grandma says is true, those hunters are still around.

That popular witch museum in town—one I've never been allowed to visit because, according to Mom, it's "a hubbub of thinly veiled witch-hating propaganda based on historical inaccuracy and patriarchal undertones"—is apparently run by a family of hunters called the Descendants. She's never told me the full story, but I know their ancestors were responsible for creating the curse that would be triggered if more than three Goode witches were inside town lines at once. None came close to breaking the three-witch rule for almost three hundred years because of constant vigilance and "good family planning."

Then I came along. Goode ol' number four.

We pass Aunt Jodie's room—temporarily empty since Grandma, Mom, and me make three—and come to Mom's room. Last on the left.

My suitcase and Tupperware are stacked by the door next to a brass four-poster bed covered in a patchwork quilt. Baby-pink paint coats the walls, but you can barely see it for all the posters of swoopy-haired boys in double denim and the shelves of twinkling pageant sashes, trophies, and crowns.

"Wow," Fatima says. "Your mom won all these?"

"Yup." I take the flower crown out of my pocket and place it gently in the middle of the nightstand, then lift my container of macarons for Fatima to see.

But she isn't paying attention. With gentle fingers, Fatima strokes the diamond tip of Mom's very first Cranberry Crown—the one that started it all. "I signed up for the pageant weeks ago. Nana let me design the costume all on my own, and he's been putting it together ever since." She turns to me. "Are you competing?"

I shift the cookies in my arms, eyes on the floor. "It's not really my thing."

Fatima shrugs with a smile and prances over to browse the ancient CD collection on Mom's desk. Fatima embodies all the good words on a pastry recipe—dainty, elegant, petite. The perfect piece of green-tea-lavender cake with whipped almond icing and served in queen's-visit-only china.

I'm a wad of spit you sidestep in the food court.

The bees in my hive rear their ugly heads. I hug my cookies closer, and the kiss of baked sugar drifts up and curls around my nose. Too sweet for the bees to handle. They melt away.

"*This* is my thing," I say, and thrust the container out.

Fatima peeps in and squeals. "Oooh, I love them! You are really, really talented! Did you make them all by yourself?"

"Sure did. Wanna try one?"

"Yes, please!"

I hand her a cookie and she eats it in a single bite.

And *this* is the part I love. The moment sugar coats their taste buds, the way the emotions play on their face. Eyes roll back, shoulders relax, the corners of their lips curl. The feeling that for a single moment, you created something that made someone else happy. I live for that.

"Mmm. So good," Fatima says, catching a crumb with her tongue. "You'll place for sure."

"Thanks," I say, mind lighter than it's been in days. I snap the lid in place, slide the macarons on the nightstand, then bounce down on the squeaky bed. "I really liked yours too. Very experimental. Judges like stuff like that, you know."

Fatima continues her tour of the room, lifting a plumeria candle to her nose. "I hope so! I love my monster cupcakes. Or really just monsters in general. They are literally my favorite thing ever."

"That's so cool. Is your pageant costume scary?"

She gives me a wicked grin. "You have *no* idea."

I laugh and lounge back on the pillows. "You gonna wear it trick-or-treating with your family?"

"No." Her face falls into a gloomy pout. "Ammi and Abu—I mean—Mom and Dad—don't really get the whole 'monster' thing. They think it's kinda weird, actually. That I'm kinda weird."

My insides hollow, and I tug a wayward string from the bedsheet. "Like you don't belong in your family."

Fatima nods. "But Nana's great. He's researched monsters and myths from all around the world and writes all his findings down in a huge book he bound together himself. He sorta passed the hobby down to me."

"Why do you call him Nana?"

"Oh." Fatima laughs. "It means my mom's dad in Urdu. That's what we speak at home. Nana's from Pakistan."

"Cool. So my grandma would be called . . . ?"

"Nani!"

"Nani Goode," I say, relaxing again. "I think she'll like that."

Fatima's smile grows, and she turns toward the open closet. She straightens the sleeve of a worn letterman jacket with a bat stitched on the collar, and glances back with an approving look. "Vintage. Nice."

I nod and smile, trying to act like I knew Mom played softball all along.

Footsteps stop outside the door and Mom pokes her head in. "Addie, your grandma *insists*"—here her tone turns sour—"I see the town festival before I leave, so grab your coat and we'll head out in a few minutes. I'm driving, since Jodie has Grandma's truck. Oh, and, Fatima—your grandpa says you can come with us if you want."

"Oh yeah, that would be great!" Fatima says.

Mom grins, then her eyes slide to the rows of crowns and go misty, in that far-off way adults get when they think about the good ol' days.

One thing's for sure though: She's never looked at me the way she's looking at those tiaras.

My fingers find the flower crown on the nightstand. I brush its delicate petals as bees hum a mournful tune in my chest.

"Why not just leave now? I know you want to," I say.

Fatima looks away, obviously feeling awkward, as Mom crosses her arms.

"Maybe I wanted to spend time with you, Adelaide. You know, before I leave for three months. Thought that would be nice. But I guess not."

Mom whips down the stairs, Fatima on her heels. She stops at the door and twists to me, voice unsure. "Um, ready?"

I touch the velvet flowers once more, and honestly, I don't know why I do it—it's very un-villain-like—but at the last second, I tuck the crown into my hoodie pocket.

I give Fatima a reassuring smile, a little embarrassed by my outburst. It's really not her fault she walked into all my family drama.

"Ready."

3

TWO HOURS UNTIL ABANDONMENT

Despite everything, the festival's pumpkin pie is as delicious as I remember. Notes of cinnamon and nutmeg dance together on my tongue in a perfectly tasty tango. Nothing could make me forget how sucky this situation is, but the whipped cream helps.

The four of us sit inside one of the jumbo dining tents pitched around town square—all of which are slightly smelly and decorated with cheesy cobwebs and plastic spiders. Fatima, on my left, shovels mac and cheese into her mouth and chatters about the lack of vegetarian options at her middle school. Across the table, Mom and Grandma are pointedly not talking to each other. Grandma's chatting ticket prices with Mr. Next-Table-Over while Mom keeps checking her phone, as if waiting for a message to pop up and save her. She just can't wait to get away.

I clench the flower crown in my pocket. Then eat more pie. I'm only human.

A big glob of it lands on my arm, and not having the emotional bandwidth to resist, I lick it off.

Giggles sound across the tent. Another person may not have heard them, but big girls are attuned to mean-laugh frequencies like we have a radar duct-taped to our foreheads. Sure enough, loitering against the canvas flap, two boys sit watching me, a bag of peanuts between them. The blond one with a rather unfortunate bowl cut points from my pie to me, snorting like a pig to the delighted laughter of his friend.

A weird tingle moves over my skin, all the way to my fingers. Probably my bees prepping for attack. I jam my lips shut so I don't stick out my tongue or say something nasty, then angle my chair away from them. I'm definitely *not* hiding, no matter what it looks like. And besides, it's not like it hasn't happened before. I've been a pro at the sticks-and-stones thing since I was six.

Sort of. Maybe. Okay, okay—it still hurts a *little*.

The cherry on top of a perfect day.

A man in a Cubs jersey stoops into the tent, the name ROY stitched over the back of his hunched shoulders. He looks like the boys—same blotchy, white skin and pudgy nose. Probably their dad or uncle. He taps the boys on the back and gestures toward the street. When the boys ignore him, he grabs their arms.

Bowl-cut boy rips himself free. "Get off me! *You* don't get to tell me what to do!"

His rat-faced friend nods in agreement.

The man tries one last time to get them to follow, but the boys turn back to their peanuts, aiming their shells at the back of a little girl's pigtails. The man sighs in defeat and slumps outside. As soon as he's gone, the boys burst into laughter.

"Pathetic. He's last in the family order. Too soft to even butcher a chicken, and he thinks I'm going to take orders from him?"

I have no idea what he's talking about, but I really, really hate bullies.

But not a minute later, a different man rips back the tent flap. He looks like a relative too—and this one's even got their mean eyes.

The man pinches the boys' ears and tugs them from the tent, whisper-yelling the way adults do when they don't want to cause a scene. They stumble back, spilling their peanuts and yelping words Mom would ground me for even *thinking*. Then the tent canvas slaps shut, and their cries are lost to the festival commotion.

My bees hum in contentment at the instant karma, but, again, I'm not going for supervillain vibes, so I let myself feel a little bad.

Besides, no matter how crummy my family is—and we are, like, serious crumb-cake level crummy—at least we aren't like *that*. I like my earlobes just the way they are, which is attached, thank you very much.

After a half hour, Grandma finally turns away from Mrs. Such-'N'-Such, who's deeply concerned about the hygienic properties of the apple-bobbing station. "Was it good, girls?"

"Delicious," Fatima and I say at the same time.

Grandma leans down with a conspiratorial eyebrow waggle. "Wait till you see the rest of the festival."

We pitch our trash and head out to the street. Noticing Mom isn't behind us, I turn.

"Yes, hi, Mrs. Peters," she says into her cell, cupping the wind from the speaker. "I'm just wondering if you had a moment to go over the details for my temporary housing . . ."

There's a squeezing in my chest, like someone trying to pipe icing from my heart. I check the time on my watch—12:27 p.m.

One hour and thirty-three minutes until Mom leaves for the airport. One hour and thirty-three minutes until she's gone for three months, and she *still* can't even give me her full attention.

"Come on, Addie!" Fatima calls, pointing toward the face-painting line. The smile on my face is stiff as fondant, but I keep it pasted on anyway. Mom isn't taking away my only chance of making a friend too. With a giant exhale, I follow Fatima and Grandma into the street.

Even though it's midday, town square is lit up with every string light, candle, and jack-o'-lantern in a two-hundred-mile radius. Even the cobblestones glow. A breeze heavy with the scent of funnel cakes whips over us, sending the army of blow-up Draculas and Caspers into a sky-borne pirouette. Pets dressed as hot dogs chase their tails, parents share gossip, and sticky-mouthed toddlers smack their lips around pumpkin-shaped lollipops. Everyone is having the time of their lives.

Except me. Because one hour and twenty-eight minutes, now.

Half an hour later, leaves crunch as Fatima emerges from the face-painting tent. The glittery ghost on her cheek is stretched by her grin.

"It looks good," I say, but my voice sounds off even to me.

As if she can feel all the emotions blender-whirling inside me, Fatima shares a small smile, takes my arm, and tows me across the festival. "I asked for extra sparkles."

"Ooh, girls! Look—the bake-off tables," Grandma calls from ahead. Her hay-filled bun seems to wiggle with excitement. "Let's check out your competition, shall we?"

We race over to the submission tent. I scope plates of cookies, cakes, and candies with a baker's eye. None of them have the steady pipe-work mine do, and none are nearly as creative as Fatima's cupcake design. Aesthetically, we should have this in the bag, but half the score is based on taste, so I can't count anyone out yet.

I find my macarons on the table labeled DEADLY DELICIOUS COOKIES AND CANDIES. I spit on my finger and shine up my name tag real good before nudging the whole container a *tiny bit* more in front of the others. It's not really cheating, just strategic. I think. Either way, my henchman bones purr with delight.

On instinct, I turn to call for Mom to look. She leans against the tentpole, phone still glued to her ear, doing that fake-phone-laugh thing adults do when they are trying to convince the other person they are more pleasant than they actually are.

The words die in my throat, and with a metaphorical shove, I bury them six feet under in a coffin so tightly chained not even the All Hallows Eve Moon can resurrect them.

"Wow," Fatima says, gazing into the field behind me. I turn, and despite my mood, I recognize "wow" is right.

A stage towers above the park with plastic gravestones jutting up like teeth across the floor. Streamers loop-the-loop around the stage's set lights, which project hordes of dancing ghosts on the theatre walls. A fog machine belches smoke, cobwebs string the black curtains like pearls, and the "Monster Mash" drones from some speakers offstage.

Below, women with poofy hair and sparkly blazers sit behind the registration table, clacking their fingernails on the sign-up sheet to draw in last-minute contestants.

"Sign up for the Miss Preteen Scary Cranberry pageant! Everyone—and I do mean everyone—will be watching tonight! Get your small-town fame right here!"

I turn away, but not before I see Mom glance up from her phone, eyes shiny with nostalgia and wistfulness and all that other gooey stuff that turns my stomach sour.

Of course *that* would get her attention. My hands clench

into fists, and I have to recall the memory of pumpkin pie to unwind them.

In the airplane-movie dog tragedies, there's always a point when the dog says—or barks—something to the effect of *My day can't possibly get any worse*. This is usually when Fido finds out that the car ride isn't to his favorite sniffing spot—dog park—but in fact on the way to the pound. The kill-shelter kind.

Now, as a self-proclaimed professional airplane-dog-movie watcher, I can say with 100 percent confidence that this is the point at which it *always* gets worse. The lesson here is never to say these fatal words.

"My day can't possibly get worse," I say anyway, stomping into the next tent. Gruesome monster masks leer from every surface. Fatima, tearing her eyes from the stage, squeals as she spots the disgusting things. She follows me into the tent, puts a rubbery clown face over hers, and cocks her head in the display mirror. Her eyes shine through two bloody slits above a mouth stretched with sharpened teeth.

"What do you think?" she asks.

"Very you," I say.

She angles her chin so the bloated cheeks catch the light.

"Well, its jaw could use some serious blush, and I think I might add some glittery eye shadow, but I think this guy is perfect for my collection."

With a flash of sequins, she flounces off for the register, the mask tucked protectively under her arm. I stare after her, mouth open. *My collection.*

She's one of a kind, that Fatima.

"Find anything you like?" Grandma asks. Repulsion curls on her face when she sees the masks. She clutches her purse tighter, as if afraid the faces will jump from the wall and try to steal her Tic Tacs.

"Nope. Just Fatima," I say, pointing to the checkout table. The cashier hands Fatima her mask and receipt, which she snatches up with so much excitement she nearly topples the old lady in line behind her.

"Oh—sorry, Mrs. DeDiggle! Addie! Nana is going to die when he sees—"

But before Fatima can finish, a squawk cuts through the air and my face is pinched by clawlike fingernails.

"Adelaide Goode!" the old woman says. "Oh, Bee, you didn't tell me your granddaughter was in town! How much you've grown!"

I bluster and squirm, but her talons sink deeper into my cheeks, smooshing my lips between her liver-spotted hands. I'll probably never have feeling in my face again.

"Mrs. DeDiggle! I didn't see you there," Grandma says. "Yes, Addie is staying with me for a little while."

Mrs. DeDiggle, apparently, is not only the type of person who sharpens her fingernails to points but also the type of person who only speaks in exclamations.

"That's so wonderful! The more the merrier! Oh, Addie—can I call you Addie? Do tell me you'll compete in the costume pageant tonight! My nephew Collin is competing, and I can't *wait* until the show! They are announcing the winners at midnight, you know! Extra spooky!"

The cashier gives Mrs. DeDiggle her total for the witch's hat on the counter, and as she's momentarily distracted, I'm able to rip my cheeks free. Massaging my numb skin, I'm about to tell Mrs. Dagger-Nail-DeDiggle she most certainly *cannot* call me Addie, but a stern look from Grandma quiets me. Mrs. DeDiggle hasn't seemed to notice though—she's digging in her coin purse, distress growing on her face. She gives an appeasing smile to the pimply teen behind the register.

"Sorry—I know I have a twenty in here somewhere. Or at least I thought . . ."

The boy pops his bubble gum, unamused.

There's a slight tug of magic, a gentle whoosh of sunshine.

"Did you check your pockets, Doris?" Grandma asks. "Sometimes I forget I put things in there and find them weeks later. It's a wonderful feeling."

Mrs. DeDiggle blinks, face flaming. "Oh, no, I'm sure I didn't—" But she slips her hand into her coat pocket anyway. Eyes wide, she pulls out a crisp twenty-dollar bill. "Well, look at that! I don't even remember putting it in there! Thank you, Bee!"

Mrs. DeDiggle hands the money over to Pimples and I glance up at Grandma. She winks.

Grandma does stuff like this all the time—bringing cheering potion to a depressed neighbor (disguised as herbal tea), curing Mr. Hick's corgi of cancer. When I visited five summers ago, she even used a spell to keep the town's historic Bogger's Bridge from collapse with a flick of her fingers. *What's the point in having magic if you don't use it for good?* she'd said.

I would normally agree, but my cheeks still sting.

"Is there a problem here?" a deep voice says to the cashier. A tall, burly white man in a police uniform comes to a stop in front of Grandma, resting two massive fists on his holster.

If this man were a recipe, his ingredients would be as follows:

1. A pinch of petulance

2. A dash of intimidation

3. A heaping spoonful of sneer

He just looks plain *mean*, and trust me—big girls know a bully when they see one.

"Not at all, Officer Hern," Grandma says, voice cold. Mrs. DeDiggle, gathering her change, looks back and forth between the two of them, then, with a nervous laugh and a quick goodbye, rushes for the exit. The cashier too seems in a hurry to get away, suddenly busy arranging plastic fangs at the other end of the counter.

Officer Hern's gaze shifts to Grandma and tightens. "Bee Goode. I see you're still in town. It's almost like you never leave." His words are dark, meaningful. That's when I know who he is.

A Descendant.

It's as if an ice cube slides down my shirt. I shudder, moving closer to Grandma's side. At the tent flap, three other men—relatives, from the looks of their shared curly hair and gaunt cheekbones—glare at us. One is muscular with a twitching mustache, and the other two—I start—are the ones from the tent. The man with the Cubs jersey and the professional ear-puller with mean eyes.

Grandma's tone is casual, but she puts a firm hand on my shoulder. "I stay or leave as I please, Ridger."

"Of course. But feel free to leave anytime you want." Ridger's stare skirts down to me, then, with a frown, he looks out the tent. Mom's staring at us from the middle of the street, lips white. Her gaze flicks from Officer Hern to his gang of cronies, and something very strange passes over her face. Something dark.

The air thickens as the other Descendants notice her. The jersey-wearing Hern makes a sound between a hiss and a choke. It sends another ice cube down my spine with the first.

They're counting Goodes.

Officer Hern hasn't taken his glare off Mom, and when he speaks, his tone is dry. "This Candice's girl?"

Grandma's nails dig into my arm as she steers me away. "Good day, Officer Hern."

"I'll be patrolling town tonight for the festival. You know—making sure rabble-rousing kids don't get up to no good. Making sure no *lines are crossed*. I hope you'll do the same." With a knife-sharp glare, he turns out of the tent, shouldering his jersey-clad family out of the way to lead his pack. Jersey-Hern barely notices, craning his neck back to gawk at us.

Grandma tugs me away until I'm tripping over my feet.

I might have been pretending to be a henchman, but I'm pretty sure I just met a real supervillain. Anyone who could get under Grandma's skin like that—the most powerful witch I know—is someone I don't want to be around.

My heart pounds very fast as we move farther into the festival. Fatima didn't seem to have noticed the exchange at all. She's busy describing a hypothetical fight-to-the-death match between all the Lord of the Rings monsters to Mom, who seems to only be half listening.

"Smaug and the Orcs are fierce, and the Nazgûl have those poison swords, but Gollum? Now, he has *drive*. Ooh, look! Caramel apples!"

She sprints off, tugging her frilly purse from her shoulder. I fall in step with Mom.

"Who were those guys?" I ask.

Mom snaps out of her reverie. "No one."

"They were obviously someone. Why were they staring at you like that?"

"Let it go, Addie."

"Are they Descendants?"

"Addie—"

"Do you know that Ridger guy?"

"I said let it go!" Mom thunders.

I stop dead in the road, festivalgoers grumbling around me.

Mom never yells. Especially at me. Especially especially not in public. She also never walks away when I'm upset, yet as she huffs away in a fury of red curls and peplum, it feels like more than just her body leaving. Like I'm being abandoned in more ways than one.

Tears burn my eyes, but my bees fly up to wipe them away. Their wings beat a rhythm of war against my heart, and I clench my fists, letting their thump take over.

After that, I don't remember any of the rides we ride, prizes we win, or booths we visit.

All I remember is Mom walking away. And how angry I am at her.

An hour later, the four of us are in the parking lot of the Dig-In Diner, a local restaurant perched right outside the town line. Fatima chatters on about her younger siblings, soccer team, and mosque as Grandma listens with occasional *mmm-hmm*s and *uh-huh*s, back pointedly turned away from her daughter. Mom, on the other hand, checks her phone screen every thirty seconds.

"I swear, if Jodie makes me miss my flight—"

"If you're worried, just go," Grandma says.

"And leave you to deal with the Herns alone?" Mom whispers. "After that display?"

"I'm more than capable of—"

A horn honks, startling us all.

"Oh good," Grandma says in a relieved tone. "She's here."

I peek out from the curtain of hair I've pulled over my glasses. Sure enough, an old blue truck idles across the street, just inside town lines. I can almost make out Aunt Jodie's dark hair behind the windshield.

So, here's the anti-curse-enacting plan: I'm supposed to go back into Cranberry Hollow with Grandma, Jodie, and Fatima in the truck while Mom and Legs—safely outside city limits—head even farther away to catch her flight. So simple and foolproof even I can't mess it up.

If Fatima thinks it's weird my aunt parked across the street, she doesn't let on. We cross the road, pausing to look both ways, before stopping in the grass in front of the WELCOME TO CRANBERRY HOLLOW sign. Aunt Jodie cuts the engine and slides out of the truck, flicking a cigarette butt under her boot and crushing it. She looks a lot like Mom, but with dark hair to match the bags under her eyes.

"Addie. You've gotten taller," she says in lieu of a hello.

If it isn't clear, Aunt Jodie's never liked me very much.

Her frown deepens as her eyes crawl to Mom. Neither speaks, but they pass a glare around like a game of hot potato.

Grandma and Fatima walk past the welcome sign, over the invisible town line. Grandma stops beside Jodie and turns, gaze somewhere around Mom's knees. "Well—ah—good luck with the new job."

Mom nods, readjusting her purse strap, her eyes on the ground. Without another word, Grandma opens the truck door for Fatima, and they haul themselves inside. Jodie follows, leaving me and Mom to say our goodbyes.

We stare at our shoes in silence. A cold wind whips over my

arms, raising goose bumps. A dog barks in the distance, and with each passing moment my bees hum louder, a familiar anger rising like dough under my skin.

Then Mom closes the distance between us, wrapping me in a hug. "I love you, Addie. You know that, right?"

I can't move my mouth. My bees have control of my clamped lips, and my arms are locked at my sides.

Mom pulls back. Hurt shines on her face as she tries to catch my eyes, but the bees seem to have control of those too. I find the loop of the floral crown in my pocket and clench it tight. Because if I don't hold tight to it, I'll grab Mom. And if I grab Mom, I may not let go.

Her nostrils flare. "I know you're mad at me, but can you please be a little more grown up about this? I'm not going to see you for a while, and I'd like my daughter to actually hug me back."

Maybe it's her tone or the heat or the never-ending hum of bees in my ears, but it's suddenly all too much. The no-magic, the curse, the fat taunts, the glares among my family, the way Mom is Fido-ing me. It boils over until all I want is to make her taste the smallest bit of the pain burning inside. And so, I find the words and let them swarm from my mouth.

"Just because Grandma abandoned you doesn't mean you can do the same to me."

She stiffens, but I don't care, I don't care, I don't care. Not about her flight or her job or the stupid, stupid curse. I won't let her leave. I wrap my arms around her, take a step back, and drag her with me.

Right over the town line.

Mom stumbles, catching herself on my shoulders. Her eyes go wide. Terrified. *"Addie, what have you d—?"*

A wave rumbles up from the ground. People scream and fall. For a moment the sky turns green, then something like lightning ignites in my chest. It rips the breath from my lungs, sucks the blood from my veins. And there's darkness. So much darkness. Endless. Unyielding. It coats every part of my body like tar.

Then, as quick as it hit, the feeling fades. I fill my lungs with air, limbs shaking. Strangely weak.

Grandma and Aunt Jodie stumble out of the car, calling our names. Fatima follows, eyes round as coins. "Adelaide. You're— you're glowing!"

I glance down. A fine green light pulses from my body, almost as if it's radiating from my bones. I jump back, throat clenched, blood racing in my veins. Breath spills from Mom's lips as she scans me, toes up, until her gaze comes to rest on my face. Fear courses off her in waves, so much so that I feel her magic pull unconsciously off mine to restore her balance.

Trembling, I glance up and my vision tunnels across the road to the Descendants walking from the festival. The heat of Officer Hern's glare bakes my skin, paralyzes me. Then a smirk breaks across his mouth, and he and his three cronies duck into his police car.

Dread mounting, I look from my glowing skin to the slash of dead, smoking grass behind Mom. The once-invisible town line.

The line that all four Goode witches are now inside.

4

THE HUNTER

Darkness. Everlasting, delicious darkness. I had grown used to nothingness all these centuries.

But no more.

> *When the fourth witch calls and the hour is nigh,*
>
> *bend thy bones to the dark wind's cry.*
>
> *A descendant's body to cloak thy form.*
>
> *A cleansing, a purge to perform.*
>
> *Find her now, thou wicked demise.*
>
> *And rise up.*
>
> *Rise. Rise. Rise.*

A body calls to me. The Descendant who will share his skin,

molded to my will. He curls his fingers, wiggles his toes, and lets me ooze into his body like poisonous slime. Magic rolls through his bones, the darkest kind. A power not at full strength until the moon rises, but growing stronger with each breath he takes—no, *I* take. For the Host's body is no longer his, but mine.

Hunger strikes in my gut like a cobra. A bloodlust. A burning, bleeding, ravaging hunger.

Hunger for *her*.

As one, our eyes open.

Rise. Rise. Rise.

5

FIVE MINUTES SINCE I RUINED EVERYTHING

The Styrofoam cup of cider trembles in my hands. Every part of my body is achy, like someone took a meat tenderizer to my muscles.

Grandma led us down to one of the picnic tables set up in the town square. Tent workers and townsfolk bustled around hanging banners, inflating balloons, or dunking apples in vats of steaming caramel. Luckily, everyone seemed too preoccupied with whispers of "gas line explosion" or "earthquake" to notice the green glow of my skin. It's less obvious now in the afternoon sun than it was an hour ago. You have to make your eyes squinty to see it.

Fatima sneaks another look at me, but I can't meet her gaze. She probably thinks I'm a freak now. The thought sends worms wriggling in my gut. It would've been nice to have at least one person in Cranberry Hollow who wanted me here.

Not that I can blame any of them. If it weren't for me, maybe they wouldn't all hate one another. Mom could have lived the life she always dreamed of. Not to mention that I'm the magical embarrassment of the family as the only Goode witch in two centuries that can't even turn a toothpick into a sewing needle.

Oh, then there's the teensy little fact that *I just activated a curse.*
On purpose.

I sorta didn't think it through, but Mom was all that was real to me in that moment. Much more than some stupid curse. And if I'm being totally honest—like, deep-dark-down-never-admit-this-to-anyone honest—I don't regret it as much as I should. Mom's still here.

Maybe that means I'm a little more villain than I thought.

"Well, what's the plan?" Jodie asks, ripping a chunk of Styrofoam from the lip of her cup.

Mom clears her throat. "I'm taking Adelaide back to the city."

Something like hope wiggles in my chest, and I glance up.

"You know you can't leave," Grandma says darkly. "The curse clearly states—"

"Forget the curse, Mom, this is my daughter! If she's in danger—"

60

Grandma sighs. "I mean Adelaide *can't* leave. None of us can. The curse forms a boundary that keeps all witches inside the city line while the Hunter searches—"

My cup slips in my sweaty hands. "Hunter?" I ask just as Aunt Jodie says, "Mom," a warning in her eyes as they flash to Fatima.

"It's okay, I—I won't tell," Fatima says, breathless with excitement. She's basically bouncing on the bench like a Pomeranian. "I knew something was going on when I saw Addie glowing. And"—she suddenly looks guilty—"well, there was this one time I was helping with the rabbits and I saw you yelling at Stephanie for getting into a basket of your magical herbs. She was the size of a walrus by the time you coaxed her down from the ceiling. I just *knew* right then you were magical, Ms. Goode! But only in the good way. You help people. Like my nana and his garden, right?"

Grandma blinks at her, momentarily stunned.

A curt laugh breaks the silence. Aunt Jodie drains the last of her cider and smashes the cup flat on the table. "Well, she was going to figure it out anyway with you cozying up to her grandpa."

Grandma's neck goes food-coloring red. "I am not 'cozying up' to her grandpa—"

"*What Hunter?*" I yell.

Silence falls, then Jodie glares at Mom. "How much have you told her?"

"Enough."

"Enough that she's prepared for what's coming for her tonight?"

"*What's coming for me tonight?*"

"Jodie," Mom growls. She rests a hand on my arm, but I don't feel it. No one ever said anything about a hunter.

Aunt Jodie's laugh is a dark, mean thing. "What, do you keep secrets from her too? I thought that was something you saved just for us."

"*Jodie—*"

"I'm just saying—maybe if you told Addie how serious this was, she wouldn't have goofed around and pulled you over the line."

My stomach plummets.

"*Stop it, girls,*" Grandma hisses between clenched teeth. "We need a plan if we're going to survive the night. And to survive the night, Adelaide needs to know what she's up against."

Mom's mouth shuts with an audible snap and Jodie scowls, arms crossed. Fatima's eyes are wide with manic glee like she's costarring in her own monster movie. And maybe she is.

On the other hand, my body is prickly and numb, anticipation and dread squaring up in a street fight under my skin.

Grandma folds her hands on the table and leans forward, very businesslike. "How much do you know about the curse, Adelaide?"

Hot and cold rack my body all at once like an undercooked Hot Pocket. I swallow, but the Hot Pocket seems stuck in my throat too. "Um, only three witches can be in town lines at once, but at least one Goode has to stay for all our magic to continue? I don't know. It started with witches and hunters a few hundred years ago."

Grandma nods, taking on the air of someone about to tell a very unpleasant story. "Witches and hunters lived by one code for generations: protect your family, extinguish your enemies. The fighting lasted decades, with massive amounts of casualties on both sides. The witches, however, were fewer in number, and by the end of the seventeenth century, they had been poached to near extinction. Only the three strongest witches were left. They called them the Unburnt for their iron grit and perseverance."

"The Goodes," I whisper. Grandma nods.

"The hunters, weary from years of bloodshed, promised to let the sisters live if they agreed to never swell their numbers past three within the town lines. You see, the hunters knew the basics of Kindred, how family is the foundation for the magic. They knew the more relations a witch has to tap into, the stronger the connection to their ancestors is—which you well know is where our magic comes from. Having only two blood relatives to fuel spells would keep the witches weak, and therefore controllable.

"To make sure this happened, the hunters forced the witches to create a curse. If a fourth witch was ever born in the village, or crossed town lines while three others were already inside, a dark creature would awaken at nightfall, inhabit the bones of a Descendant, and hunt once more."

Chills erupt as the creepy singsong spell plays through my head again.

> *Evil devours.*
> *You've nowhere to flee.*
> *When the Goode witch numbers*
> *err over three.*

"With the powers of a dark pendant," Grandma continues, "the creature would be drawn to the bones of the fourth witch and suck her soul within the stone. Legend has it that if the fourth witch's soul is absorbed by the pendant—"

Mom grabs Grandma's arm, face livid. "*That's enough.* God, Mom—you're freaking her out!"

And she's probably right. Even my bees are hiding in their hive, too afraid to come out.

Grandma grumbles and slips her arm free, but adopts a lighter tone. "But the witches were cunning. They added two loopholes to the enchantment: The Hunter could only rise for one night until midnight before being banished back to the darkness; and while in his hunter form, the Hunter would be devoid of a face so that he couldn't use his senses to detect the witch. He must rely solely on the pendant to find her."

Grandma unclasps her hands and leans back, weary. "So the curse was cast, and for centuries the Goode line endured, never swelling past three. All the while, the Descendants have kept a . . . tentative peace with us."

"Until now," Aunt Jodie says.

"Until now."

Dread falls on me like an anvil in one of those old "back in my day" cartoons. Of course I would be the Goode to doom the family. My Curse Regret-O-Meter ticks a little bit higher.

"What about my glow?" I ask.

Jodie squints and tugs my wrist close to her face. "It's almost like—"

"Like her bones are glowing," Mom says, voice high.

"It's how the pendant tracks her," Grandma says. "Like calls to like. The curse turned her bones into whatever material it's made out of."

"Glass," I say, and as unlikely ingredients melting together to create a perfect recipe, it all comes together. How my body feels hard yet fragile all at once. Like I could shatter from the inside out at any moment.

For a moment, everyone stares at me, open-mouthed. Mom's hand hovers, like she wants to give my shoulder a comforting squeeze, but stops when I pull away. I can't handle being broken in any more ways.

Her hand falls into her lap, her face tight. "I still don't get why the curse chose Addie. I was the last to cross the line."

Jodie's glare is so hot, it bakes my face. "Maybe because she pulled you over *on purpose*. Strong intent can sometimes sway the bonds of magic."

Mom turns. "Why, Addie? Why would you do this?"

Because I was scared. Because I didn't want you to leave me. Because I'm twelve and Mrs. Plebert told our science class that brains aren't fully developed until twenty-five.

But mostly—because I've never been Goode enough.

I don't say any of that. I just jam my mouth shut and look away.

"Which Hern do you think the Hunter will choose?" Jodie asks.

"Definitely not James or Levi," Grandma says. "Those two have cabbages for brains. Corbin's away at college, and Mathius is only twelve, so I doubt them. There is that one who works at the auto shop—Roy, I think?"

"No, it won't be him," Mom says. "He's—"

"Wimpy?" Jodie offers.

Mom glares at her, and Grandma nod-shrugs in agreement. Then her face turns dark. "It's Ridger I'm worried about."

No one says anything, but we're all thinking the same thing. It has to be him.

Mom glances to Grandma. "We need a plan."

Grandma brings her shoulders up to full height. "The Hunter doesn't start his hunt until nightfall, so we have time to prepare. We go back to the house and do the strongest protection spells we know, then hunker down for the night."

Mom and Aunt Jodie burst in outrage.

"I will *not* spend the evening with her—"

"Mom, I don't think—"

"*Listen*. All of you," Grandma spits, spectacles flashing dangerously. "We need to work together if we're going to survive the night, which means yes—Jodie, Candice—you will cast protection charms over the house *together*. Sister Kindred has always been best for protection; you know that. And neither one of you have the strength needed to ward the town, so that falls to me."

"What about my nana?" Fatima asks, concern on her face for the first time.

"I will make sure you and your nana are the safest on the block. Now," Grandma says, rising, "let's clean up and get started. We don't have too much time before the Hunter picks a Host, and it's going to be a long night."

Me and Fatima take our time throwing away the empty cider cups and napkins while the adults bicker just out of eavesdropping range. All the while I can't shake this weird, muted feeling. It's like when the TV's gone fuzzy and the volume is cranked on high until you can't remember ever hearing another sound but the static. My bones give a vicious ache and I hiss.

Fatima puts a hand on my shoulder, her delicate brows wrinkled. "You okay?"

I nod, rubbing my forearm. Then a crash echoes to the left, and Fatima and I both jump. Onstage, the Miss Preteen Scary Cranberry pageant banner hangs limply from a single rope where it's fallen to the ground. Workers scramble to reattach it under the furious screams of pageant officials and beehive-haired mothers.

Fatima's face falls. "Well, looks like the pageant's out now. Nana's gonna be so disappointed."

I jolt. To be completely honest, I forgot the costume contest with everything going on. With an unexplainable urgency, I fumble in my pocket for the flower crown, needing to hold it. Relief spreads as my fist closes around the wood, but something jabs into my thumb. Hard. With growing dread, I glide my fingers around the circlet. My stomach drops when I feel a split in the wood, the crown's two halves hanging by a single, limp piece of wicker.

I broke Mom's crown when I pressed her into me. When I tugged her across the town line. When I enacted the curse.

Maybe I'm being extra metaphoric with my impending doom around the corner and all, but it feels like my chance of ever proving myself Goode enough broke right down the middle with it.

6

THE HUNTER

Old house. Old hate.

It sits like oil on the Hunter's tongue. Or really, the Host's tongue, but the Hunter has control of their body now. He licks their lips greedily, feeding off the room's misery.

The Hern Manor and Witch Museum is perched atop Cranberry Hill, but no mortal can see past the colonial columns and sweeping gardens. No one but the Hunter can *hear* the song. How each brick sings of hate, how each stone whispers despair, or how the floorboards echo the cries of the burning.

For this is the noble, ancient house of Hern. Of warriors. Of witch-hunters.

The Host squirms inside the Hunter, deep in the Dark Place where he was shoved once his body was chosen. His thoughts bubble up to the Hunter, not yet used to this new arrangement, but not wanting to complain either. The Hunter pats his chest where he imagines the Host lies. *Worry not, my friend. When evil is slain and I take my rest, thou shalt be the hero remembered.*

The Host stills. Satisfied, the Hunter glides toward the sitting room, where his family waits for him. Shallow sunlight wavers through the moth-bitten curtains, but soon the moon will rise, and with it, the Hunter's full powers. His fists flex in anticipation.

Beyond the cracked door, angry whispers echo. The Hunter leans close to listen.

"I can't believe *he* was chosen. Out of all of us!"

"It should have been me," says a child's voice. "Even if his powers don't come in until nightfall, he could use me as his host to keep an eye on those maggot-bitten witches. It's not like they would expect a kid to get picked."

"Yeah, 'cuz you're too small," says a deeper voice. "No one wants to live in the body of a squirrely, pimply twelve-year-old."

"My pimples are a genetic predisposition! I am *not* wimpy!"

"Are too."

"Am not!"

"Are too!"

"Silence!" A wizened voice bites through the air. "The Hunter—in the Hern body he's *rightfully* chosen—will be here any minute. I expect you all to behave."

Heat courses through the Hunter's body. A blaze of anger at being questioned. A desire to strike, crush, and burn swells within him. But no—he cannot. These are Herns. Loyal servants. Remembering hate, passing it down generation after generation.

Keeping *it* safe.

And the Hunter does not forget family. He was the first Hern, after all, truest of his name. Slayer of seven and sixty witches. Loyalty to the family name is just as important as slaying.

The Hunter brushes his fury aside like cobwebs and steps into the room.

An old man sits like a king on a throne beside an empty fireplace. His white skin is liver spotted and he's tufted with pale hair, but the Hunter is drawn to his eyes—black and cold and full of delicious, delicious hate.

"Your Darkness," he says. "We've been awaiting your return for a long time."

He snaps his fingers, and a horde of Herns emerge from the shadow—his sons, nephews, and grandsons—and rush to one of the many display cabinets behind him. A boy with hair the shape of a poison mushroom brings the Old Man something small lying on a pillow. He takes it from the boy, snaps again, and the child shrinks back against the peeling wallpaper.

"I believe you will need this."

On the pillow rests a large crystal pendant. A glint of red flashes in the Hunter's eyes as he picks up the ancient chain and loops it over his neck. As the pendant settles on his chest, the stone glows green.

Power climbs up the Hunter's body like poisonous weeds. He smiles, letting the darkness take root in what little soul he has.

"We have kept it safe over three hundred years, waiting for the day you would rise and deliver our town from the Unburnt."

It is hard for the Hunter to rip his gaze from the pendant, but he does only to look at his family. For the first time, the Hunter speaks, his voice cold as breaking glass. *"Witches burn, but family is forever."*

"Witches burn, but family is forever," the Herns echo.

Pride slithers in the Hunter's gut. "There is work to be done."

7

SIX HOURS UNTIL MIDNIGHT

After dropping Fatima off at her nana's, we get home and hunker down for what Grandma is calling Operation Bunny Bunker.

"I survived 'Nam; I'll survive this," she says, and wiggles her fingers, causing the ceramic lawn bunnies to snap to attention. In groups of three, they begin to circle the perimeter of the house, their ears twitching in time to their marching hops.

Cold wind whips over the porch, raising goose bumps on my arms. The night stretches its fingers, staining the sky like spilled coffee. My senses play a paranoid I Spy—every shush of a passing car, a ghost; every breeze through the wildflowers, a predator.

I shudder, and Grandma notices. She bends down and locks my chin in her fingers until I meet her eye. "Listen to me, Adelaide. Now—WWAGWD?"

What Would A Goode Witch Do? It's one of our weird family sayings along with *a gargle of vinegar a day keeps evil spirits away!* and *toadstools before bed, morning breath's a dread.*

"Be brave," I say weakly.

Grandma pats my cheek. "When Goodes stick together, Goodes survive. We *will* get you through this, Adelaide."

I nod, trying to ignore the voice in my head that's saying, *But I'm not a real Goode.* Inside, my bees are arming for war. I spilled the metaphorical potion, so I should be the one to clean it up. I just haven't found the right mop yet.

Glass shatters as two bunny sentinels crash together, spooking us both. What's visible of their legs and tails wiggles upside down in the wildflowers. With a sigh, Grandma snaps her fingers, and the bunnies repair and spring to their feet. Satisfied, Grandma opens the door, and we go back inside.

Ramus, Pickles, and Petunia are at our feet in an instant, whiskers twitching and snooters sniffing. I bend down to pet their ears when angry voices rise from the living room.

". . . Well, let's try again."

"We've tried four times, and I'm sick of holding your sweaty hand."

"Oh, very mature, Jodie."

"Ancestors, give me strength," Grandma says under her breath, and with a look like she's charging back into the swamps of Vietnam, she marches us into the living room.

Mom and Aunt Jodie stand across from each other, red-faced and huffy, with what looks like a fuzzy Hula-Hoop whizzing around their ankles. I squint, and the blur materializes into a frenzied horde of rabbits, circling excitedly from the raised voices.

"Why isn't the Bubble Wall charm up yet?" Grandma demands.

When they see us, Mom uncrosses her arms and Aunt Jodie scratches the back of her neck, eyes averted.

"Can't get it to work," Aunt Jodie says.

"Of course you can get it to work," Grandma says, stomping forward and snatching their hands in hers. "You're *sisters*. This is what your magic was meant for."

"We haven't been sisters in a long time," Aunt Jodie grumbles.

Mom gives a *tch* sound, but I think Aunt Jodie has a point. Maybe their relationship is so broken they can't even do sister Kindred anymore.

"The line again," Grandma says, and closes her eyes. Begrudgingly, Mom and Aunt Jodie follow suit.

Magic sparkles in the air as their voices lift in unison.

> *"Sisters, mothers, daughters,*
>
> *hear our call:*
>
> *Keep us safe with your protective wall."*

There's a sound like the air being ripped apart, and pressure builds until my ears pop. Outside the window, a purple, jiggly bubble falls over the house in a dome. Grandma frees her hands and peeks out the blinds. "No human but a Goode can cross that line—Hunter's Host or not."

For the rest of the evening, the house is a flutter of motion. Mom bewitches the rosebushes so the blooms sway on their stalks, flashing their spiky, thorned fangs at passing flies. Aunt Jodie brews a bitter-smelling potion that, if thrown, will temporarily make the victim move at turtle speed. Even the rabbits chomp their wicker toys menacingly as if sharpening their teeth for battle.

Despite the show, everyone's on edge. We pace around the house, snapping at one another like peanut butter brittle. The truth is no one knows which will be stronger—the Hunter's powers or the Unburnt's Kindred. We'll only find out once he gets here.

Which is why I'm sitting in the bay window, kneading at my magical cherry pit. If I could *just* get this magic thing down, maybe I could help save the people I love from this mess I've made.

I glance at the darkness gathering on the horizon. It's late enough that the Hunter could be on the lookout at this very moment. The thought turns my stomach, and I press harder, digging invisible fingers into the shell that binds my powers.

He will *not* have my family.

But for some reason, the shell feels harder than before, made of stone, not husk. Even when I do find a fissure and pull, my bones give a nasty throb and the magic slips through my fingers.

As if sensing my anxiety, Rosie jumps up on the cushion with me and settles onto my thigh, purring her rabbity purr. I rub her ears as the slightest bit of tension leaves my muscles.

"Well, that's all we can do for now," Grandma says, emerging from the hall pink-faced, with hair falling from her bun. "I'll make some tea. Maybe something to calm the nerves?"

I nod, and she gives me a tight smile before bustling to the kitchen. Mom's and Aunt Jodie's footsteps echo behind her amid a wave of hushed bickering. For a moment, I lose myself in the gentle plush of Rosie's fur.

Then from the kitchen comes a slam, a scuffle, and a muffled scream. Heart pounding, I jump to my feet, knocking a surprised Rosie to the floor.

"What is that?" Aunt Jodie asks.

"It's a raven!" Mom says.

I ease around the hall on soft feet, resting my head against the kitchen door to listen. Rosie follows, ear perked flush to the wood.

A screeching bolt slides open, then comes the heavy pulse of fluttering wings. Clawed feet slap on laminate countertops.

"It's carrying a message," Grandma says. "Look at its leg."

There's the sound of rustling feathers followed by the crinkle of unfolding paper.

Then utter, unbearable silence.

"What does it say?" Aunt Jodie asks.

Grandma's voice is leftover-soup cold. *"Give up the girl and no one gets hurt. Fight, and all of you will die."*

My heart is a lump of dough in my throat. I'm too scared to move. Too scared to breathe.

"The Descendants know where we are," Mom says, a tremor in her tone.

"Of course they know where we are," Aunt Jodie snaps. "Your

daughter has a curse-GPS tracker in her bones. I swear, Candice, if you and that kid of yours could have just stayed away—"

My heart plummets, and from outside the door, I can practically hear Mom's jaw drop in outrage. "Do you think I *wanted* to come back?"

"Obviously not. You've always done everything you can to get away from us."

"Will you two give it a rest?" Grandma says wearily.

"It's not like I was wanted here," Mom says. "The moment I got pregnant, you two started making plans to ship me away."

That gets Grandma fired up. "What did you want us to do, Candice? Have us all stay here together as a happy family? You, me, Jodie, Adelaide, and the Hunter—who, mind you, would have risen the moment Adelaide was born inside city lines. I 'shipped you off' to save your lives."

Mom's voice rises an octave. "I wanted you to come with me! Move as a family, stick together, like family is supposed to. I was a child for God's sake, alone and pregnant and shipped off to raise a magical kid by myself."

"This might be shocking, but it's not all about you, Candice," Jodie spits. "You know at least one Goode has to stay in Cranberry

Hollow for magic to survive here—did you want to be the one to explain to seven-year old Brayden Cartwell that his brain tumor came back because you thought your comfort was more important than his life? How about the faulty water line we mended just in time so the whole town didn't get poisoned? This town depends on our magic."

Mom sputters as Grandma cuts her off. "Speaking of, if I had left, I would have had to sell the Goode Witch and the sanctuary, and then there would have been no money to feed that 'magical kid'—as if Adelaide can really do magic in the first place—or for you to have a sitter so you could go to college and make something of yourself. *I did all that for you.*"

"Money and magic weren't what I needed. I needed a mom."

For a moment, numbness skewers me to the spot. Then angry footsteps rattle the floor beams, and I have two seconds to scurry across the hall and throw myself onto the couch. Mom charges in, eyes like thunderclouds. A cup of tea floats beside her, but her magic is so saturated with anger the surface boils and snaps. "Come on, Adelaide. Bed."

Meekly, Rosie and I follow her up the steps even though it's super early, taking care not to get too close to the hissing cup.

I crawl into bed, still in my jeans and sweatshirt, but Mom doesn't even notice. She perches on the edge of the mattress, eyes closed and breathing deep, no doubt going through the *72 Steps to a Calmer You*, or whatever her newest half-read self-help book suggested. The teacup careens to a stop on my nightstand as Rosie hops on the bed, circles five times, and then flops into the plush quilt.

I run my finger over her back and jam my eyes shut, because maybe if they are closed tight enough, the words can't get in my head. But of course, they seep through my ears instead.

—if you and that kid of yours could have just stayed away—

—as if Adelaide can really do magic in the first place—

The words taste like burnt coffee, all bitter hues and ashy grounds. Hearing the truth out loud proves everything I've suspected—I'm a walking plague, an obligation to the family, the stain everyone tries to 409 up, but I'm puked-up spaghetti sauce. And that, sister, is not coming out of the carpet anytime soon.

The chunky truth remains that I activated the curse to keep Mom with me, and even though we're all stuck in this house together, I've never felt more abandoned.

Mom puts a hand on my shoulder, and I jump. Anger dissolved, her expression drifts into something pale and sheepish. "How much did you hear?"

I shrug her off and nestle farther into the covers. "Not much."

"So . . . everything." Mom deflates into the pillows beside me. She stares at Double-Denim Boy on the wall for a long time, absently fiddling with the chain of her necklace. Even her expensive blush can't hide how strained she looks.

The ache grows in my chest, but not for me, for her. I can't help it—she's my mom and I still love her. No matter how little she cares about me.

I shyly rock my shoulder against hers. "Hey, are you guys okay? That was . . . bad."

Her smile is wax-paper thin. "No. We haven't been for a while, but that's not for you to worry about. The point is to keep the Descendants *out*, at least until midnight. We'll all work together until then. I promise."

"And after that?"

She tucks a frizzy lock of hair behind my ear. "We'll see, Addie. We'll see."

I glare. The thing is I've been in this game for twelve years.

By now I've learned when adults say *we'll see*, it translates into an answer you *don't* want. And in this situation, *we'll see* means Mom is still leaving for her job once she's cleaned up my mess.

Still, the idea of her going up against a monster sends my bees scurrying for cover.

I have to *do* something.

"Why do they hate us so much?" I ask.

"They're scared, I guess," Mom says. "Few things are as fearsome as a woman who embraces her power. And I suppose over the centuries the hate just stuck."

I nod, brow crinkled. "Do you think it will be Ridger?"

"I'm not sure. I knew all of them growing up, you know. The Hern boys. There was Greg—he was the squirrely-looking one—then Samuel, he's got that stupid little mustache now, then Joseph, Josiah, and Roy . . ." Some strange emotion flits across her face, but when I do a double take, her expression is hard. "But Ridger worries me. He—well—let's just say I've seen him be violent in the past."

The memory of his face crawls over my mind again and I shudder. I can tell Mom's afraid of him, and not in the he-might-be-possessed-and-come-for-my-daughter type way. More like the I-know-his-dark-secrets type way.

And that fear sparks a memory. The memory of another fear, something so silly now.

Sign up for the Miss Preteen Scary Cranberry pageant! Everyone—and I do mean everyone—will be watching tonight! Get your small-town fame right here!

Hope hopscotches in my chest as a new plan takes shape.

Because if I'm on that stage in front of everyone, then the Hunter will know *exactly* where to find me. And if he's hunting me, he'll leave my family alone.

Sighing, Mom slaps her thighs and rises to her feet. "Well, drink your tea and try to get some sleep. It'll be morning soon, and all this will be behind us." She bumps her lips against my forehead and pads across the room. At the door, she turns to make sure I drink my tea.

I grab the cup and press it to my lips, pretending to swallow. But I have no intention of sleeping. Or putting my family in danger a moment longer.

I might be an obligation, a curse, a blight on this family, but this is *my* family. And no one is going to hurt them on my watch.

I might get hurt. Heck, I might get my soul sucked out, but some things are worth the risk, right?

And maybe, a little voice whispers in the back of my mind, *this sacrifice will prove what I couldn't before—that I deserve to be in this family.*

8

THREE HOURS UNTIL MIDNIGHT

Slipping out was surprisingly easy. As soon as Mom left, I grabbed my backpack and started shoving things inside. I don't know why I packed half of what I did. It wasn't like my tablet, the clown mask Fatima left in Grandma's truck, or the broken shards of the flower crown were going to save my life, but I just couldn't leave them behind.

I was halfway up on the windowsill when Rosie gave a thunderous thump with her back legs. Swiveling around, I found myself on the receiving end of her reproachful glare.

"It's going to be dangerous, girl," I said, stooping down. With a defiant snort, she leaped into the open pouch of my book bag. Her head popped up a moment later, and clamping the drawstrings with her front teeth, she tightened the cords around her like a seat belt.

"All right. It's your funeral," I said, and threw the bag over my shoulder, because who was I to stop an independent woman from making her own life decisions?

Climbing out the window was painless. Sneaking past the ceramic bunnies, a picnic. Shimmying down the drainpipe, a piece of cake. But now, as I stare at the dark night through the warped edges of the Bubble shield, my feet stick to the ground.

Doubts echo—those boys' mean laughter, Mom's yells, Aunt Jodie's and Grandma's hurtful remarks.

I teeter on the edge of the glittering sphere, half a mind to run back inside.

A rummaging sound comes from my bag, then Rosie's head bursts out near my shoulder, something dangling in her mouth. I reach up and grab it.

The broken pieces of the flower crown.

Right. I *can* do this. I'm a Goode, for goodness' sake.

I give Rosie a quick peck on the cheek, clutch the crown to my chest, and march through the barrier.

It's like trudging through a thick wall of Jell-O. The goopy, purple membrane oozes between my fingers as I push through, everything distorted, slimy, and smelling slightly of cranberry juice. When I flop out the other side, the entire force field jiggles with a deep *wong-wong-wong*. Without a backward glance, I skitter across the driveway and over the lawn.

Crisp wind howls through my hair as I creep down the wooded lane. My neck cricks from glancing over my shoulder so much, and I quicken my pace, breath coming fast. When I pass a neighbor's jack-o'-lantern, I swear I see its glowing eyes follow me.

I'm doing this for Mom. I'm doing this for Grandma. I'm—

"Psssst!"

I jump so hard Rosie crashes to the bottom of my book bag. I glance around, but there's only a small one-story house with a sprawling front garden. The house looks vaguely familiar, but it's not until I catch sight of the faint Bubble Charm that I recognize where I am.

"Pssst!" Fatima calls, frantically waving from an open window. An angry Rosie pops her head out to click her teeth at me, but at the sight of Fatima, her ears perk and her whiskers twitch.

Half-curious, half-annoyed, I run to the window, galumph through the Jell-O ward, and crouch behind a rhododendron bush. *"What?"*

"Come in! Quick!" Fatima says, eyes darting in the dark behind me.

Sighing, I clamber through the window and land on my butt. Pain bursts up my spine, stealing air from my lungs.

"Addie, are you okay?!"

"Yeah," I say through gritted teeth, massaging my backside. "Glass bones. I think I've gotta be more careful."

Concerned, Fatima helps me to my feet. With gentle fingers, I prod the bottom of my spine and stretch. Nothing feels broken, but what a close call.

Meanwhile, Rosie has wiggled out of the bag and circles Fatima's pink-slippered feet. With a hushed squeal of delight, Fatima scoops her up and cuddles the bunny to her chin.

Hakeem's living room is warm with a lazy fire licking the grate and squishy maroon armchairs along the walls. Billowing plants drip from their pots—organized in neat lines on nearly every flat surface—and the smell of heavy spices and fresh naan perfume the air. Any other time I might have found it all comforting, but my heart beats a little too fast and my bones hurt a little too much to relax.

"How did you see me?" I grumble.

"Well, you're sort of glowing," Fatima says.

I glance down at my hands. The lightest bit of green rises from my skin, like a telescope view of stars in our solar system. It definitely wasn't this bright earlier.

"And anyway, I've been keeping an eye out," Fatima says, tugging the camera strap looped around her neck.

My mouth pops open. Of course she would be glued to the window all night, waiting to snap a monster picture like some kind of weird, paranormal paparazzo. Strange as it is, the thought curls my mouth into a grin.

Fatima doesn't return my smile. Instead, her eyes cut, suddenly suspicious. "What are you doing out here anyway?"

I consider lying, but then I remember how honest she was about her parents with me.

"I'm luring the Hunter away from my family."

She crosses her arms and cocks a hip. "So, you're giving yourself up?"

"Well, yeah," I say, fingers toying with the strings of my hoodie. "It's what I have to—"

"I thought Goodes weren't supposed to give up. That you guys were the 'Unburnt' or whatever."

"Look, it's more complicated than that." My bees awaken and flutter under my skin. "I don't want everyone to die because of me. If he sees me up on the pageant stage, he won't be able to hurt my family at home. He'll come for me there instead."

"Wait—you're doing the *pageant* to lead him away?"

"Well, yeah."

"And what about all the innocent people in the audience?"

To be honest, my brain hadn't got that far yet. "Um, I'll work it out as I go."

A strange, manic fire lights Fatima's eyes. "What if you didn't have to? What if there's a way to fight? Would you do it?"

I stare at her, wary. "What do you mean?"

A grin splits her face, dissolving all traces of disappointment. "Follow me."

We tiptoe down a dimly lit hall. The scent of cardamom and masala blooms as we pass the empty kitchen, and despite my growling stomach, I frown.

"Where's your nana?"

"He's downstairs putting the finishing touches on my costume. I didn't have the heart to tell him I couldn't do the pageant. But don't worry—he won't bother us."

We pad into a low-lit prayer room. A single beam of moonlight falls on a massive Quran, propped on an ornate stand, and catches the folded corner of a gold-threaded prayer rug. Elegant scripture hangs in frames on the walls, and a coatrack is layered with tasseled scarves and tiny round caps.

After handing Rosie off to me, Fatima drags a chair to a bookshelf in the corner, climbs on, and pulls down the topmost volume. She returns cradling a leather book with binding so frayed, some of the loose pages have been stuck back in at odd angles. Mysterious markings swirl over its cover—not quite English, not quite Arabic. But what's inside is even more mysterious.

Fatima thumbs through the tome in a blur of fangs, talons, scales, and slime. Monsters haunt every page, creatures from all corners of the globe. Some beasts I recognize, like the Pegasus and a kraken, but others—a terrifying boney thing called a wendigo and the half-lion, half-scorpion manticore—I've never heard of. I'm drawn to a depiction of a particularly curvy mermaid brandishing gleaming blades, when Fatima speaks.

"This is a collection of all the creatures Nana's learned about on his adventures around the world. It's my absolute favorite! There's Domovos and jinn, merrows, and gumihos, plus so much more! Even"—she turns to a page in the back—"spells that break any curse."

Numb, I take the book and devour the words before me.

A SPELL TO BREAK ALL CURSES

Brew in a pewter cauldron under undiluted light of the moon:
1. A tear of a babe
2. Twice-swallowed belladonna
3. Dragonfly drool

Repeat the incantation:
"By life, by death, by love, I demand to unmake, this curse and its binding, now break, break, break!"

Author's note: Legend says even with the proper ingredients and incantation, only the strongest magic can break a curse. Results may vary.

"Do you think this will work?" I ask, mouth dry with excitement.

"It's worth a shot. Especially if the only alternative is giving yourself up."

Something light and warm bubbles in my chest, sweeter than any cider. It's the feeling of reaching into a dark cabinet for a jar of canned spinach and finding a cupcake instead. *This is it.* This is the way not only to save my family but also to prove myself as a Goode. Heat blazes up my body, magic crackling in my fingertips.

Plus, I really, *really* didn't want to wear a pageant tutu.

"Can I take this?" I ask, gesturing to the book.

"Sure," Fatima says. "We're gonna need it with us to kill the Hunter."

"We?" My eyes flash to her. "No way!"

"Addie, come on! Let me come with you! All my life I've wanted to find a real monster. And I bet I know more about mythical creatures than anyone you know!"

I cross my arms. "Oh yeah? Like what?"

"Like the fact that all monsters are allergic to cranberries! It's their number-one weakness."

My mouth falls open. I quickly shut it. "Really?"

"Really. It's on page 283." Fatima turns to the page and points at the illustration. Sure enough, a distressed hag runs from a group of villagers pelting her with small ruby spheres.

Huh. Maybe that's why my ancestors chose to settle here. I make a mental note to ask Grandma about it the next time I see her again.

If I see her again.

"See? I can be useful to you. Let me help! Pleasepleaseplease pleaseplease!"

"Okay, okay," I say, throwing up my hands. "You can come. But it will be dangerous, and I'm not making any promises we'll both survive."

Her eyes blaze as she tightens the ends of her sparkly hijab, like a knight adjusting a helmet for battle. "Oh, I'm ready."

I slide the book into my backpack, followed by a slightly disgruntled Rosie, who looks at Fatima's arms with a desperate longing.

For the first time, Fatima's face pinches with concern. "But where are we going to get all these ingredients?"

Now it's my turn to smile. "Ever been in the back room of the Goode Witch?"

9

THE HUNTER

They stand in front of the window—the frizzy one, the one whose bones call to the Hunter like an ache behind his ribs, and the mortal girl who cradles an old book like it's a treasure.

Bushes tickle his nose as the Hunter crouches in the shrubs, as close to the house as the spell will allow. The only thing that can pass the protection bubble are Goodes and animals, which was why the Old Man sent the raven.

Silly, to try to plead. The Hunter plans to kill them all anyway. He'll take pleasure in the way their souls sing as he tears them from their wretched bodies.

For night has fallen and he has a witch to hunt.

10

THREE HOURS UNTIL MIDNIGHT

We ease out the window, plop down in the bushes, and skitter down the drive. A sound echoes to my left and I yank a squealing Fatima behind the mailbox.

"Shhh," I say, ears alert. My heart throbs in time with my bones; my eyes dart in every direction. There's silence for a moment, then gravel crackles on the road and headlights appear.

I exhale. It's only a car.

A beam of moonlight breaks through the clouds, illuminating CRANBERRY HOLLOW P.D. painted on the side. My heart skips a beat. Officer Hern is barely visible through the tinted windows, but I can just make out his curly hair and sour expression as his eyes rove over the trees.

Palms slick, I settle deeper in my hoodie to dim my bones.

Fatima twists herself into a human shield to cover the glow, but she's skinnier than me, so it doesn't help much. Still, the gesture makes me feel a little less alone.

As the headlights pass over our hiding place, I count my heartbeats.

One, two, three . . . one, two, three . . .

For a moment, I'm sure his eyes find us, but the car inches down the road until he's out of sight.

Breath leaks from my chest. "Let's go," I whisper.

After many failed attempts in which we both get bruised and a lot of goo in our ears, we learn the only way to transport Fatima past the Bubble Charm is for me to burrito-wrap myself around her and fling us through the wall. Finally free, we creep along the trees in silence for a long time, Fatima vibrating with excitement. Seriously, the girl is bouncing down the trail like there's Pop Its in her shoes.

"Go on," I say.

"What?"

"I can tell you want to ask me something."

Her words come out in a squealy rush. "This is all just so cool. Magic is *real*. I knew it. I just knew it! You have to tell me all about Kindred! Please please please!"

I huff a laugh. "What do you wanna know?"

"Anything! How does it work?"

"Uh, well, Kindred is the magic family shares. The more members you have and the closer you are to them, the stronger the spells."

"So you can do magic too?"

My cheeks burn. Of course I remember doing magic—on the rare occasions I could tap into it. The feel of Grandma's warm hand wrapped around mine. The whoosh of electricity as our Kindred connected. The ancestors' gentle whispers, soft as fairy floss.

"Sort of," I say. "I'm . . . well, I'm really weak. We don't know why, but it probably has something to do with the fact that this is a family-based magic system and everyone in my family wishes I wasn't a part of it."

"Oh, Addie," Fatima says, playfully swatting my arm. "I'm sure that's not true."

I shrug, suddenly engrossed with my hoodie's drawstring.

Fatima redirects the conversation. "I heard your grandma say something about sister Kindred?"

I sigh. "Each family relationship specializes in different kinds of magic. There's sister-sister, which is the best for protection spells; mother-daughter, which is best for run-of-the-mill daily tasks; and soul-mate Kindred, which is good for healing. Plus about a hundred other types."

"What about father-daughter Kindred?"

The string rips free with a snap. I toss it on the ground and smoosh it with my sneakers. "I think that's good for undoing. Fixing mistakes, spell reversals, that sort of thing. But I haven't tried it. I . . . never knew my dad."

"Do you know his name?"

"Nope," I say, popping the *P* with pretend indifference. Then I snort. "There was this one time I was—ah—snooping in Mom's closet and I found this old box with all her things from high school. Across the front of a diary was scrawled *C hearts R 4ever.* So, I guess I have a first initial."

Fatima laughs. "I thought people only did that in movies."

The tree line is replaced by music, lights, and a chattering hum as we hit town square. In the shadows, we skirt the edge of the festival, dashing over cobblestone streets and striped-awning storefronts, across the magically enhanced Bogger's Bridge, and through the alley separating Grandma's shop and the Rotten Cranberry bar.

The Goode Witch is a tiny, slightly crooked shop, as if the building fell into a snooze on its neighbor's shoulder. The storefront drips in vines, tinkling wind chimes, and stained glass lawn ornaments. THE WITCH IS IN sign, which usually glows neon pink during store hours, now hangs lifelessly behind the finger-smudged window. Channeling big henchman vibes, I snake my hand inside a plastic black cat figurine beside the welcome mat where Grandma hides her keys, and with one sneaky turn of the latch, we're in.

I loved coming here as a kid—partly because Grandma would let me play with the cash register, and partly because I was convinced the shop was a secret fairy den. Even now, as I step inside and the scent of lemongrass and musk kisses my nose, that childlike, dormant part of me rears its head, wanting to believe.

Everything is cluttered and green—the walls, the overflowing plants. Even the air, textured and humid, stirs images of spongy moss and pine needles behind my eyes. Rows of gleaming crystals promise clarity and good fortune, a two-for-five deal on incense assures spiritual cleansing, and customers can predict their futures if only they purchase one of the laminated astronomy charts hanging haphazardly on the walls.

Most of the bells and whistles are for the tourists though. The real magic is in the back.

"Come on," I say, and slip behind the counter, holding back the beaded curtains for Fatima. She gasps as she steps into the back room.

"Whoa."

The back room looks a bit like a walk-in closet, if a walk-in closet held magic instead of Birkenstocks. Everything whirls, bangs, or sizzles at irregular intervals. Shelves of wriggling plants sway on their vines—two even look like they're locked in a thumb war. A long cabinet stands next to them, overflowing with glass bottles, vials, and jars, brimming with potion ingredients. A mini cauldron bubbles merrily in the corner, emitting fumes in a zigzag pattern, the telltale sign of a giddying potion. The vapors whisper up my nose as I pass, and I'm seized with an overwhelming urge to giggle.

"What do we need again?" I ask, grinning in a way that I'm sure makes me look like a goon.

With a dopey grin herself, Fatima heaves the monster book out of my bag and thumbs through its pages while Rosie hops free to sniff around. Fatima finds the ingredients and flips the book around.

1. A tear of a babe
2. Twice-swallowed belladonna
3. Dragonfly drool

"Does your grandma have all this stuff?" Fatima asks, eyes rising with the potion shelves stretching to the ceiling.

"Let's find out. You start right, I'll start left."

"Got it," Fatima says, and marches to the first row. Rosie follows after her, immediately busying herself by nibbling on the shelf corner.

On the opposite end, I run my finger over each yellowing label. Rosewater. Adder's tongue. Pickled hemlock. Fermented cat turds. Blech.

But of course, Grandma's supply never fails. Within five minutes, Fatima locates the tear of a babe and dragonfly drool, which are almost identical except for the fact that the drool bubbles in its vial like a lava lamp. It's unfortunately me who finds the twice-swallowed belladonna, a single black berry on a twisted vine, suspended in yellow-brown bile. Dinner churns in my stomach as we walk back up to the front counter.

Fatima arranges the bottles in a glittering line. Her eyeball is comically magnified as she stoops down to inspect them. "Now what?"

"The spell says all the ingredients have to be stewed," I explain, fumbling in a drawer for matches, "then an incantation is said over them, and—"

Something cold drips down my spine. Something dark. Something *wrong*. I freeze, waiting, goose bumps erupting like fireworks on my skin. Then a force like an invisible fishhook latches around my chest and pulls the air from my lungs. My bones burst with bright, green pain and I crumple to the ground with a cry.

"Addie!" Fatima yells.

The front window shatters. I throw my arms over my head as glass rains down. Fatima screams. Rosie bolts under the counter, only the quivering puff of her tail visible.

I brush glass off my face, eyes darting through the window. The tall silhouette of a cloaked figure lurks just beyond the wreckage. At his chest gleams a brilliant emerald pendant.

The Hunter.

"Fatima, run!" I say. Glass crunches as I stagger up. The pain is so disorienting, so overwhelming, I'm not sure if it's from the window or my bones.

Lurching forward, I swipe the vials off the counter just as the Hunter leaps through the window. His movements are too graceful, too light. Inhuman.

He prowls forward, puffs of shadow steaming from his feet, his hands, his shoulders. Every step closer seems to suck more strength from my body. The pendant wakes with a wicked pulse, and my bone-glow dances in time with its light.

I'm so tired, so scared. I sag against the wall, too weak to move. He looms closer, close enough that I smell the rank stench of decay. By a fraction of moonlight, I see the legend is right—under his hood where his face should be is instead an undulating black shadow.

My mind goes white with pain.

"*Weak . . . Unwanted . . . Unloved.*"

The words hiss through my brain with a voice unlike anything

I've ever heard. Somehow deep and thunderous, but high and cold. I grab my head to keep it from splitting. The vials slip through my fingers and glass tinkles below. I claw for the cherry pit of my heart, desperate for magic, the only protection spell I know seizing my mind.

"Away thou beast, not one step more; my ancestors come, and they bring war!"

But the Hunter looms closer. He cups the pendant, cradling it closer to his body. My chest lurches forward, drawn to its dark powers.

"A-way thou beast, not one step m-more . . ."

The cherry pit stays closed, and my panic rises. I can't crack open the shell, can't feel the sunshine. I scratch, pry, tear, and stab, but nothing happens.

"*I can end it all. Thy grief and suffering. No one would mourn you anyway. Not the mother who abandons you. The grandmother who doesn't have time for you. The aunt who finds you a burden . . . Let me ease your pain . . .*"

I cry out as another throb jolts my body. There are tears in my eyes as I shake my head, refusing to listen. But some part of me shatters. Shatters at hearing the truth.

Anticipation crackles off the Hunter in waves. He lifts the pendant closer, inches from my skin—

Then something whistles by and cracks into the Hunter's shadow-face. An earthy, green scent blooms as he recoils, cloak sizzling where the substance meets his skin.

"Addie, move!" Fatima yells, and launches another vial.

I collapse just as the bottle sails past. The Hunter twitches and crumples, staggering for the window. A blur of white flashes by as Rosie scampers through my feet, grabs his cloak with her teeth, and pulls. Fatima sends a third vial airborne and the Hunter trips and rolls out the window into the night.

"What was that?" I ask, limping to my feet.

"Mama Tutu's Shredded Mustard Green Evil Repellent. Found it on the 'dangerous' shelf," Fatima says. She rushes forward and pours some of the tiny herb flecks into my hands. Rosie appears at her side, teeth bared, and together we inch toward the window, mustard green repellent at the ready.

As if rising from the grave, the Hunter stands, patches of his cloak burnt and frayed. If he did have eyes, they would be boring into mine. Just when I'm sure he'll attack, he turns and, with a whirl of his cloak, vanishes.

I slump against the cash register.

"Addie?" Fatima asks, lifting her hand to my forehead as if checking for a fever.

My whole body shakes. "Th-the ingredients. I dropped the bottles. I—I think they're broken."

Fatima rushes over to where I stood when the Hunter attacked. Silence rings like a bitter aftertaste, and I know the truth. Fatima shuffles back holding a cracked but overall intact bottle of twice-swallowed belladonna.

The dragonfly drool and tear of a babe, however, lie shattered on the ground in a tiny puddle, half seeped through the floorboards.

"Maybe there's more in the back," Fatima says, and whips through the curtains, but I know there isn't. We took all we could find.

Weak . . . Unwanted . . . Unloved.

A sob sticks in my throat as I wipe tears from my cheeks. I might have played at being a henchman, but this guy's a whole other caliber of villain. If he's Thanos, then I'm Swiper the fox.

A circling Rosie falls against my legs, trying to lick flecks of mustard greens on her back. I bend down and dust them off, feeling thoroughly miserable, when a tiny grain gets stuck under my nail. I pick it out and roll it between my fingers, and suddenly, a thought churns through my mind, silky as the richest butter.

I jump to my feet, elation swelling inside. Because I may be weak, but if this little fleck proves anything, so is the Hunter. If he can be hurt, he can be stopped.

And maybe—*just maybe*—I can save my family after all.

11

THE HUNTER

The Hunter cleans his face and hands, raw and red from those burning mustard greens. How those pesky witches learned about his weakness, the Hunter doesn't know. He spits from pain. He hates being weak and vulnerable, but nothing can be done until his powers regenerate.

The Hern Museum is silent in the way dead things are. Even the walls that echoed screams of burning witches have gone quiet. The entire manor holds its breath, waiting for the Old Man to speak.

He sits rigid in a sagging armchair, the centers of his bushy eyebrows turned down in anger. Flames stir weakly behind a cracked marble hearth, but even as the Descendants shiver around the room, no one dares to rekindle it.

Finally, the Old Man says, *"What did he let those witches do to you?"*

The Hunter continues cleaning his skin with a *brush, brush, brush*, eyes heavy on his work.

The mushroom child moves from the shadows. "You should have picked someone else. Any one of us would have been more worthy." He looks straight at the Hunter, eyes full of malice. "This Host will fail you. Take me instead, Your Darkness."

If the Hunter wasn't in so much pain, he would strike the boy like a viper. The *insolence*.

Something stirs in the Dark Place. His Host's emotions, trickling down the Hunter's spine like a velvety web of spiders. If the Hunter could, he would grin.

Yes, this Host may be physically weak, slimy, and gullible, but he has an unhealthy thirst to prove himself as a Hern. To fit in despite the soft feelings he keeps locked deep. More than anything, he wants approval.

And that makes him the most useful.

"You're wrong," the Hunter says. *"I can feel this Hern's power, his desire to please us. There is hate in this heart."* He turns to his family. The chill in his voice sends patterns of ice crawling up the windows.

"Witches burn, but family is forever."

12

TWO HOURS UNTIL MIDNIGHT

"This is the weirdest thing I've ever done," Fatima says, running a hand over the sea of bobbing red lumps in the bog. We crouch on the moon-licked shore, inspecting the waterline as Rosie scuffles around somewhere behind us—no doubt foraging for wayward cranberries.

It turns out packing my tablet was a great idea. After a quick search online, we found out most dragonflies are babies this time of year and prefer to wade in natural pools. They're also called nymphs, which Fatima just loved. Luckily for us, half of Cranberry Hollow *is* cranberry bogs, so finding the nearest water source was only a stone's throw away from town square.

And despite the fact that every inch of my skeleton feels cracked, something light takes root in my chest, sprouting hope between my ribs. If the mustard greens proved anything, it's that I can fight this monster and—with the help of the last two ingredients—maybe even break the curse.

"What?" I ask. "You don't trespass into cranberry farms in the middle of the night looking for dragonfly spit on the regular?"

Fatima giggles and tugs the monster book out of my backpack. Her thumb whirls through the pages as I survey the clearing around the lake, watching the tree line for signs of a shadow. None emerge. Even with my recent win, fear lingers like a mouthful of garlic, but I grit my teeth and swallow it down.

"Do you think we will be safe here?" Fatima asks. "You know, since monsters are allergic and all?"

I shrug. "Hopefully."

"Fingers crossed it is! Got the milk?"

I hold up the expired carton, stolen from the Goode Witch's break room. Clumps slosh inside. Somehow, I don't think the bugs will mind.

"Good. Now, the dragonfly."

I think it's worth noting that I really, *really* hate insects. There are just too many legs, too many eyes, and not enough bug spray in the world. On my fourth-grade camping trip, a herd attacked, and I woke up with exactly seventeen spider bites—some in not-so-mentionable areas. Plus, bugs caused a *literal plague*, which is something I definitely don't have time for tonight.

Half in awe, half in serious concern for her sanity, I watch Fatima plunge her hand below the surface like a champ, fingers wiggling in the murky depth. For a ridiculous moment, I imagine a scaly swamp creature grabbing her arm and yanking her below the surface. But I shake my head. Even if that did happen, Fatima would probably be thrilled.

"Ah-ha!" she yells, as her hand emerges with a splash. Dripping in the center of her palm, a tiny wingless bug blinks up at us, completely confused by its sudden change of scenery.

"Behold—a deadly sea beast!" Fatima says, bringing the bug close to her eye for better inspection. Her face glazes over in that same ooey-gooey way it had when she saw that gory clown mask. "Aww, he's cute, isn't he?"

Cute is a rather generous term in my opinion. Its body is a long, brown tube with six spindly legs jutting out the sides. A head, bulby like a Christmas ornament, shakes as if trying to wake from a nap.

My skin crawls with imaginary bug legs. "Ugh. It's gross!"

Fatima swats my arm with her free hand. "Now, that's not nice. He's not judging you for how you look."

I begrudgingly bob my head, because apparently reason disappeared hours ago.

"Here," Fatima says, sliding the baby dragonfly into my palm before I can protest. "Take him while I look up the instructions."

I hold the thing at arm's length, face pulled back in revulsion. My voice squeaks out much higher than normal. "If this thing bites me—"

"Oh, stop being such a baby. Alhamdulillah, it's the twice-swallowed belladonna that survived. Imagine having to re-create *that*. Now," Fatima says, positioning the text on her crossed legs. "We need to give him a warm sip of milk before singing him a lullaby—preferably in a high-pitched hum. A deep sleep and ample amounts of drool are guaranteed within forty-two seconds!"

"How are we going to get it warm?"

Fatima shrugs, turning the page over for clues. "Don't know. Use your breath, I guess."

Right. Of course.

The dragonfly scuttles forward in my hand, eyes up. Expectant.

Knowing I'm about to do the strangest thing I've ever done, I pop the milk carton top open and dip my pinkie inside. When I pull it out, a white droplet dangles from my finger. Heaving a breath from deep in my throat, I blow hot air over the milk, then offer it to the dragonfly.

He considers it for a moment, moving his head this way and that. Then he leans down and sucks the whole thing up in one gulp like it's a frothy, bug-sized cappuccino.

A smile peels across my face as Fatima bursts into applause. "Yes! Now quick—sing!"

My grin falters. "Sing what?"

"A lullaby."

"I don't know any lullabies."

"Well, make one up!"

I grimace at the bug, now searching the lines of my palm for more milk. I clear my throat and, with a glare at Fatima, crack out a tune.

"Hush, little buggy, don't you cry, you're a sleepy dragonfly."

"Higher," Fatima says, watching the insect's head roll back to my face.

"Hush, little buggy, don't you cry, you're a sleepy dragonfly."

After two octaves, I learn that clenching my butt cheeks helps. I push out the notes, higher and higher until my throat is sore and my ears ring. I never was a good singer—I think even Fatima's face is wrinkled into a permanent wince. But the dragonfly doesn't seem to mind. In fact, he circles five times, kneads his front legs into my skin, then curls up in the middle of my palm like a tiny house cat.

I can't tell if my ears are still ringing or if the thing is giving off a faint, high-pitched snore, but when a glittering spit bubble emerges from his mouth, triumph fills my body like a dozen balloons.

We did it! Fatima mouths. She pulls an empty vial from my backpack and, with a few careful movements, coaxes a single drop of dragonfly drool inside. She passes it to me, and I clutch it tight, my fist vibrating with excitement.

Two down, one to go.

We slip the sleeping bug onto a nest of leaves and watch him drift off into the tide of cranberries. Feeling happier than I have since activating the curse, I throw an arm around Fatima. "Well, that wasn't too bad."

She laughs and scoops up Rosie, cuddling her tight to her chest. "It was actually kinda easy!"

This is another example of a line you never want to say if you actually want things to remain easy.

It's in this exact moment that voices begin to hum through the fog. Deep and male. Figures emerge as the sharp sweep of flashlights beams through the trees and swipes over our feet. Even in the silver moonlight, the newcomers' curly hair and matching sneers mark them for who they are.

Herns.

"Run!" I yell.

We bolt around the bog and into the trees, shouts and footsteps close behind. My bones ache, but something in their lack of this-is-the-end-of-the-world intensity tells me the Hunter isn't with them. He must still be weak from the mustard greens, and the thought gives me a burst of hope, pushing me faster.

Breaking through the woods, we sprint down a gravel road, footsteps growing louder behind us. We turn along a sharp bend and almost run headfirst into a wooden fence. A sign hangs from the five-foot padlocked doors.

FARMER ANNE'S CORN MAZE
OPEN 10 A.M.–6 P.M.
TRESPASSERS WILL BE FED
TO THE SCARECROWS

"Climb!" Fatima says, and hoists herself up the wood, Rosie clinging to her neck for dear life. I follow her over the fence, my henchman résumé growing so large I could probably interview for the Suicide Squad. But on the way down, my foot slips in mud and I crash to the ground. My elbow crunches as the glass inside cracks. My vision goes white with pain.

I want to scream. I want to cry. I want my mom so badly the ache in my bones echoes through my heart.

But I'm doing this for her.

I'm doing this for them.

"Come on, Addie!" Fatima says from somewhere above me. "We have to keep moving!"

The deep voices grow closer. I bite my tongue to keep from moaning and let Fatima pull me to my feet. One arm held in the other, I limp into the maze.

Inside the wall of corn, hush falls like a curtain, almost as if the stalks themselves devour noise. Reeds press in from all sides, smooshing the air from my lungs, while crooked-mouthed scare-crows stand sentinel over our game of cat and mouse.

We take a left, a right, then two more lefts, until the ache in my arm flares so hot I double over gasping.

"We can't stop moving," Fatima pants. "They'll find us."

An unknown voice cuts through the fog. "What if they already have?"

Stalks rustle, and a boy steps out of the corn. The uneven line of his bowl cut catches the moonlight.

Ice crystallizes in my veins. The mean boy from the festival.

Fatima pushes me behind her. "Go away, Mathius!"

My mouth drops. "You *know* him?"

"He's in my grade. Nothing but a big bully." Fatima's eyes narrow as she glares back at him. "Touch us and Addie'll fry your brains with a single spell!"

I grimace. Fatima doesn't know I can't even magically toast bread, let alone fry a brain.

The boy snorts and stalks closer. "*Fat* chance. I heard she's power-less. Doesn't even belong in her coven."

I don't miss his inflection or the way his eyes linger on my middle, lip curled in disgust. It makes something curdle in my stomach, clumpier than the dragonfly milk. He's 100 percent right. Of its own accord, my good arm slinks into my hoodie pocket and grasps the edges of the flower crown.

"Well, you can't have her!" Fatima says, blocking his path. From her shoulder, Rosie bares her teeth.

"Sure, I can. I'm a *Hern*. And when I bring her in, I'll have it all—the name, the glory, the portrait on the museum wall. You stupid Goodes wouldn't know anything about legacy." Mathius sniggers. "I think I have the face for an oil painting, don't you think?" He strikes a ridiculous pose that makes him look like a very constipated bowler, before dissolving into a fit of laughter.

My spine bends as if it wants me to fold up and disappear. I try to conjure my bees, but they aren't home; a vacancy sign hangs lifelessly on the hive doorknob. Strangely enough, they all must have flown into Fatima, because her entire body jitters with rage. Like if she unzipped her coat, a million wasps might fly out the spot where her torso should be. Or bats.

Or pterodactyls.

"Why don't you just wait a few years?" Fatima asks. "I'm sure your mug shot will be much better quality."

Despite everything, I nod in surprise. Fatima might make a good henchman too.

Mathius's mouth snaps shut. A muscle twitches in his jaw, and I have about two milliseconds of warning before he pounces. With a sharp shove, he pushes Fatima to the ground and lunges for me. Mathius's arms are around me before I can move. Pain lances up my elbow and I bite back a scream. All at once my bees flood back to me, and maybe a little something else. The cherry pit in my chest pulses, and a humming like electricity flutters over my skin.

Mathius yelps, and his weight disappears. He stumbles back and rubs his forearm, eyeing me warily. Relief floods through me, not just for fighting him off, but also because the pain in my elbow has downgraded to a dull ache. I flex it gingerly, marveling at the magic. Now, if only I could *control* it.

I'm feeling pretty good about the whole situation until I look up to smirk at him and see what's looped around his arm. Then the leer melts right off my face. He notices a second after I do. With delicate fingers, he untangles the flower crown from his sleeve.

"Give that back!" I yell. My voice is thin and shrill. I lunge forward, but Mathius swings it out of reach. His evil smile returns, full force.

"Over here!" he calls. "I've found her!"

My heartbeat triples as excited voices sound across the maze. Their shuffling feet draw nearer.

I grab for the crown again and Mathius stretches higher, dangling it right about my head in his version of some sick game. Something mean and hairy glints behind his eyes, and in that moment, he realizes that whatever he has, I want back desperately.

I know what he's about to do a moment before it happens, *see* the idea flash across his face. My vision tunnels as he launches the crown over the stalks, where it soars twenty yards before disappearing into a sea of untamed corn.

My feet grow roots, pinning me to the spot. Tears clog my throat. Somewhere, as if on the other side of a nightmare, Mathius laughs. All the while, the tramping footsteps grow closer.

Fatima appears at my side, corn husks and dirt stuck to her hijab. She yanks my arm. "Addie, we've got to go!" Her fear snaps me back to attention.

"But the crown! We have to find it!"

"It's not worth your life!" She heaves me forward and I stumble down the path, the empty space in my hoodie pocket widening like a chasm.

Mathius calls after us. "Try and run, little witch. See how long it takes the darkness to find you."

13

TWO HOURS UNTIL MIDNIGHT

Last year for the Fourth of July, me and Mom made a summer berry trifle. Layers of whipped cream, ladyfingers, strawberries, blueberries, and raspberries all squished together in a crystal bowl until the contents oozed over the sides and we had to clean it up with fingers (on Mom's part) and tongues (on mine).

That's what town square feels like. A giant, stuffed fishbowl of sticky fingers and sweet, heavy smells. Children rush by in a whirl of laughs and screams. Vendors and food trucks shout out their delicacies. People elbow into one another on their way to gift stalls. I basically have to play hopscotch to avoid being jostled. If another bone gets cracked, I may not be able to handle it.

I pull my hood up to hide my glow, leaning heavily on Fatima's arm. The missing weight of the flower crown is an ache between my ribs, and my bones feel more brittle than ever, but I've got to get that last ingredient.

Unfortunately, it's at that moment I catch Mrs. Doris DeDiggle's eye in the crowd. With a sound that can only be described as an elated squawk, she comes at me, her talons darting for my cheeks. Too weak to dodge in time, I resign myself to being smooshed between her clammy hands like Play-Doh.

"Oh, Adelaide Goode! What interesting body paint! Part of your costume, I presume? I remember your mom shining like a star up on that pageant stage all those years ago, and I knew when I saw you, just *knew*, you had that spark just like she did! Oh, and Fatima! Your grandfather is hinting you will have the best costume in the show!"

Fatima's smile is tight. Her eyes dart around for a quick exit as Mrs. DeDiggle flings my head this way and that like a rag doll.

Something shiny glints out of the corner of my eye and I freeze. A police badge. Ridger Hern prowls between the milk-jug toss and pin-the-wart-on-the-witch stations, eyes roving the crowd.

Ridger's the one we need to look out for.

Let's just say I've seen him be violent in the past.

I may not be Nancy Drew, but I have a hunch that just because he has a face right now doesn't mean he's innocent. If the Hunter can disappear in a cloud of smoke, he can probably shift back between his forms at will.

A shudder passes over me and I nudge Fatima. Her eyes go round as lollipops.

"Sorry, Mrs. DeDiggle. Dress rehearsal—" Fatima says, untangling me from Mrs. DeDiggle's grasp and pushing through the crowd. We scurry over the pumpkin patch and crouch behind a rusting wagon. Officer Hern didn't seem to spot us, but that isn't very calming. He's here, which means the Hunter is already on the hunt again.

Fatima tugs my book bag off my shoulders. Rosie, fur slightly rumpled, pops up and sniffs the caramel-apple air.

"You okay?" Fatima asks, gently lifting my bad elbow.

I nod, not trusting myself to speak.

"The crown Mathius threw—it was important to you?"

I rub a patch of dirt off my jeans, suddenly uncomfortable. "It was my mom's."

Fatima's face darkens as she somehow understands all the

things I don't say. The complicated feelings about the crown, my mother, and me. I don't think I could explain even if I wanted to. "He shouldn't have done that to you."

I shrug, pretending I care less than I do. "No, he shouldn't have. But he also wants an evil spirit to suck out my soul, so I think this is the lesser of his two crimes."

Fatima bobs her head in a you've-got-a-point way before handing me the last empty vial. "For the tear of a babe. The last one!"

The book didn't give any shortcuts for this one. Just good old-fashioned meanness that hopefully results in copious blubbering. I grip the vial so hard my hand shakes.

"Let's finish this," I say.

I peer around the wagon at the crowd of costumed children, zoning in on one very plump toddler. He's got two dads, both distracted with the mayhem caused by his siblings. One dad struggles with an older sister, touching up her face paint amid her desperate bid for freedom, while the other—quite unsuccessfully—tries to coax sparkly fairy wings out of a second toddler's mouth.

"You can't eat nylon, Jennifer! How many times do I have to tell you?"

Jennifer—my target's twin from the looks of their shared

curls—crinkles her face and, with the sound of a very small, high-pitched cannon blast, disintegrates into Full-Meltdown Mode.

Even though I bug Mom about who my dad is, most of the time I don't miss what I've never had. But looking at this family, I can't help but wonder why some are lucky enough to get two dads while I don't even have one.

Fatima follows my line of vision. A wicked smile curves her lips. "Leave it to me."

She stalks forward, me on her heels. We creep around the stroller and peer down. The kid munches on M&Ms, blue and orange dye smeared on his face. Besides that, he's actually kinda cute, with curly ringlets, dark skin, and a button nose. He looks up at us with big gingerbread-brown eyes, and for a second, I almost feel bad.

Almost.

Fatima whips her hand once more into my book bag and turns, so I can't see what she's doing. When she jumps back around, I'm met with the terrifying face she bought earlier today—the clown mask, complete with bloody fangs and googly eyes—plopped right on her head.

"GRRR!" she roars at the boy, wiggling her fingers menacingly.

The toddler's eyes go wide, then he mashes another M&M in his mouth like it's popcorn and Fatima is the most fascinating movie he's ever seen.

Fatima pulls the mask up to her forehead, face pouty.

I pat her shoulder. "I thought you were terrifying."

She sighs. "Thanks."

Feet pitter up my back, then Rosie's whiskers tickle my ear. She wiggles free from the book bag, shimmies over my shoulder, and hops down on the stroller tray. The boy jolts, then claps his pudgy hands together with a squeal.

Nearly nose to nose, Rosie turns a bright pink eye to him, sizing up her prey. Then, in what I can only assume is a vicious bunny roar, Rosie's mouth stretches wide, showing every single one of her long, pearly teeth.

The toddler smacks his lips faster but *still* shows no signs of fear. Rosie's mouth snaps shut, an annoyed twitch in her tail as she turns her back to the boy. She soars into Fatima's outstretched arms and promptly buries herself in the wool of Fatima's sweater, utterly dejected.

I cross my arms and circle the stroller. "Tough guy, huh?"

The kid kicks his legs in contentment, drooling chocolate down his front. The image, however disturbing, sparks an idea.

I snatch the bag of M&Ms from his hands, tip my head back, and pour the entire packet down my throat.

So I'm not Thanos. But I think I've got this Swiper thing down.

The boy's momentarily shocked. Then his lip quivers, his face crinkles, and I'm sure I'm about to see tears when—

—the kid suddenly seems to remember he has fingers and, completely distracted, sticks at least five of them up his nose.

"It's official." I slam the wrapper down on the stroller tray. "This kid has no soul."

"Gross," Fatima says, muffling a giggle.

I push up my sleeves in frustration and notice a brown M&M clinging to my hoodie. Face hot and in desperate need of more chocolate, I plop it in my mouth.

I instantly regret it.

"BLECH!" I gag and spit the candy on my palm. Only it's not candy. It's definitely *not* candy.

I whirl around. "Rosie?! Did you POOP on me?!"

Rosie's ears slump as she gives me what can only be an

appeasing smile. Horror, revulsion, and amusement war for territory on Fatima's face, but to her merit, she doesn't laugh.

The kid, on the other hand, dissolves in hysterics. Great whoops rack his entire body, jiggling his baby chub and squeezing fat tears from his eyes.

Tears.

"The vial!" Fatima yells, but I'm already on it. Vial in hand, I catch a droplet just before it slips off his chin.

I slide the tear into my pocket as one of the dads turns around. He stares from his son to me to Rosie and Fatima and back.

"Um—cute kid," I say, grabbing Fatima and hightailing it out of there, leaving the confused dad with two hysterical toddlers.

Dodging festivalgoers, bonfires, and wayward pumpkins, we sneak around the haunted house, passing a CLOSED FOR COFFEE BREAK sign tacked to the tarp door. I pull back the canvas and we crawl inside.

If you've ever been in a haunted house, then you know what this one looks like. Smoke machines, fake blood, blinding strobe lights, and grotesque dummies everywhere. Unfortunately for us, the lights have been turned off, leaving us in semidarkness. *Fortunately* for us, the "semi" part is because my skin is pulsing with enough light to illuminate everything within a five-foot radius.

We collapse on the floor, panting and holding stitches in our sides. My bones have upgraded their pain package from an Uncomfortable Dull Throb to a Streamlined Zigs of Pain pulsing from spine to fingertips. Rolling on my back, I pull the vial from my pocket and watch the glittering tear sparkle in the light. A grin tugs my lips. The last ingredient is ours.

I pat Rosie's head, and she grinds her teeth in a rabbity purr. Fatima beams at my side. "Now what?"

I slip the vial in my book bag. "First, I swallow a whole box of Tic Tacs. Then—"

The words strangle in my throat. My bones explode with pain as a voice echoes through my head. Too high and cold. Too deep and slow. Evil.

"Then thou shalt die."

I look up into the black, gazeless stare of the Hunter.

14

THE HUNTER

Her glowing flesh calls to him. It sings the song of burning bodies, of bloated limbs, of screaming souls. What melody her soul will make as he rips it from her chest, he doesn't know. But he can't wait to find out.

He stalks forward, hands outstretched. The mortal girl with the fluffy vermin on her back scurries for the vial of mustard green leaves, but he is ready. Just as she tosses the flecks of green, he whips out the contraption the Old Man gave him. Its top opens like a mushroom and the herbs patter and slide off the top like rain. Not a bleeding drop touches the Hunter. His Host, deep within him, echoes his satisfaction.

The Hunter smiles behind his shadowed mask and lurches forward.

"Addie . . ." the mortal says, fear prickly in her voice.

Fear. The scent clings to the girls like rust and rot and glorious decaying things. The Hunter breathes deep as they back to the wall.

Then the witch pulls the mortal girl behind her. "Hold my hand!" she shouts, and closes her eyes.

"Away thou beast,

not one step more;

our ancestors come,

and they bring war!"

Magic saturates the air, putrid and foul. Blue wisps smoke from the witch's hands, dissolving as soon as she conjures them. Her mumbling turns frantic and her eyes wild.

But she is not enough, and she knows it. Her weakness fills the room the way poison cloaks a stomach, the way a snake holds its prey in a deadly embrace. The Hunter lets each curl of fear caress his skin and sink into his bones.

"Weakling. Unloved. Unwanted," he chants through her mind. *"Give up now and it will all go away . . ."*

With each step forward he takes, the pendant glows brighter. The witch's skin flares green, and her eyes bulge with delicious, delicious fear. Wisps coil from her body, drawn by the pendant. Triumph surges through the Hunter as the pendant throbs in his hand. Her soul swirls closer with each breath. Closer.

A sudden blow from the side knocks the Hunter off his feet. He turns to find three women, one with tears streaked down her face. They reek of magic. The young witch gasps and collapses as the wisps of green flutter back into her body.

"No!" the Hunter screams.

Witches. The whole maggot-filled coven. Something that feels like hate coils up from the Host in the Deep Place, echoing the Hunter's own anger.

"Mom!" the little one screams, and throws her arms around the redheaded witch.

The old witch issues a gust of sparkling wind from her hands and pushes the human girl with the squirming hare out of the way. "Run straight home, girls, and don't leave the house!" The old witch turns to face the Hunter once more, rolling her shoulders. "We'll hold him off."

The next gust catches the little witch, loosening her hold on her mother. "Mom, no!"

With a wet, sad smile, the redheaded witch unlaces the girl's arms and plants a kiss on her forehead. "Addie, go." With her own gust of magic, she pushes the little witch toward the door.

"*No!*" the little witch cries again as she flies through the air. With a sob, the redheaded witch turns from her daughter and joins hands with her coven.

The Hunter stands, grin malicious, hand ready to strike.

Suddenly, foulness stirs in his gut. Feelings swim up from his Host—years' worth of tormented memories from his cousins and uncle, hurt at their disdain for him, and most of all, confusion at the mother's reaction. For in all his life, the Host has never once experienced a love so pure from anyone in his family.

The Hunter doubles in pain, gagging. His Host's emotions move through him like flesh-eating beetles. They surge, bite, and sting.

Then, without meaning to, without knowing how, the Host slips to the forefront of their skin. The switch is instantaneous. The mortal form of the Host sheds the Hunter's body like a snakeskin, sending him barreling to the Dark Place.

The room holds its breath. The witches pause, brows furrowed, as if sensing the change too. On the surface, his Host doesn't dare breathe. Still stooped, his face is hidden under the hood of the cloak, but his vulnerability, shock, and fear worm down to the Hunter's pit. A war rages in the Hunter's mind.

He shouldn't be able to do that. I'm the dark one. I have the power.

No, whatever hiccup comes his way, he will not let it stop him from exterminating those spell-casting toe warts.

Anger lashes through the Hunter, and he rips back to the surface, burying his Host deeper inside him than the darkest, foulest abyss.

15

TWO HOURS UNTIL MIDNIGHT

"Mom!" I scream. The Hunter stalks toward her.

Grandma squeezes her and Aunt Jodie's hands until all their knuckles are white. They begin to chant.

> *"Away thou beast,*
> *not one step more;*
> *our ancestors come,*
> *and they bring war!"*

Kindred sparks. Like sunshine, but far hotter. A volcanic eruption or a solar flare. My hair stands on end as an orange wave bursts from the center of their clasped hands and rushes out in a glittering, electric shield.

The Hunter hesitates a moment—maybe curious, maybe fearful. Almost delicately, he lifts a finger to the tangerine wall, caressing its surface. It gives under his touch, and my heart pings to the bottom of my chest. I can't see it, but I just *know* he's leering as he passes through the protection spell.

Grandma's lips drop into a perfect *O*, face bone-white, horrified. Her shock scares me more than anything, because I have never—not once in my life—seen magic more powerful than Grandma's. She jams her eyes shut and chants faster.

> *"Away thou beast,*
> *not one step more;*
> *our ancestors come,*
> *and they bring war!"*

Desperate, I grab Fatima and chant the lines along with them. I scream the words, because maybe if I'm loud enough, the ancestors will hear and give me magic just this once.

Just. This. Once.

Fatima squeezes my fingers and says the incantation herself, even though she doesn't even have magic. But we try.

We try. We try. We try.

The Hunter swats the last of the shield from his face like a buzzing mosquito, emerging on the other side, where my family waits, unprotected. My lungs, the room, our ancestors themselves hold their breath for a single heartbeat.

With a sound like the sky sucking up thunder—two jets of shadow whirl from the Hunter's hands. They hit my family square in their chests. Mom and Grandma fly left and crash into the tarp wall while Aunt Jodie careens right, landing in a plastic graveyard display.

They scream and Fatima screams. I think I scream too, but everything is white noise, and mean laughter, and thumping hearts, and I can't be sure it's even real. Because this can't be real. It *can't* be.

Wood planks and debris move as Mom stirs underneath. She emerges from the rubble and shoves away the dummy covering Grandma's face—eyes closed and knocked out cold.

The Hunter stalks forward. Mom struggles to her feet, stepping in front of Grandma, but the creature bats her away a second time with a wave of black mist.

"Run, Addie, ru—!"

Her head dings against the tent pole and she goes silent.

Something cracks inside me. Not my magic—not my bones—but something deeper, something raw. My vision flashes crimson, my palms tingle, my teeth grit. In an explosion of buzzing, my hive awakes, armed for battle and furious. I have no plan, no magic, and no clue what I'm doing, but I have a thousand furious bees and two meaty fists. I run at the Hunter and tackle him to the ground.

We struggle in a tangle of cloak and fury and feet and right hooks. The Hunter's hand flies up in surprise as I claw at his sleeve. It falls, revealing a pale arm and some kind of red-and-blue sports emblem in the center. Without thinking, I grab his naked wrist.

My bones flare white. There's heat, static, and light but something else too. I'm vaguely aware of the haunted house coming to life around us—lights flashing, animations bobbing, a loop of creepy laughs booming from hidden speakers—but mostly, it's the crack of the cherry pit in my heart and kiss of sunlight that overwhelms my senses.

Kindred courses through me. A different kind. A type I've never done before. Ancestors whisper like always, speaking their names and stories, filling my body with magic. But some of these whispers are new—foreign names and stories I've never heard before.

The strange whispers call me, knowing me by name, even though I don't know them. They aren't dark, or evil, or scary. They're just family.

Family.

I glance up at the Hunter, his features shrouded in shadows. But there's a human Host's face hidden there somewhere. A face I've just done Kindred with.

Breath whirls from my chest, and without meaning to, I break the connection. The spell sends us hurtling in different directions—me to safety, the Hunter over to Mom and Grandma and beyond the back tarp.

"Addie!" Fatima kneels at my side. Somewhere behind us Aunt Jodie struggles to free herself from the plastic graveyard.

"I'm all right," I say, breathless. A single word courses through my mind like lightning. *Family. Family. Family. Family.*

Laughter—real laughter, not the scary track—echoes around the corner, followed by a ragtag group of teens. They stare at us for a moment, as if expecting someone to yell "Boo!" Of course, no one does, and their anticipation melts into confusion. One particularly muscled boy rolls his eyes. "Oh, come on! These two aren't even in costume. This place has really gone downhill."

In that exact moment, Aunt Jodie—finally free—flings back the coffin lid with a roar. The boy screams, clawing his way up his companion's arms. It would have been comical but—

Family. Family. Family. Family.

Aunt Jodie's chest heaves as she kicks off spiderwebs and plastic bones, eyes darting around the room. She hauls me to my feet and whips my head side to side, looking for injuries. "You okay? Nothing hurt?"

I try to nod, but she has my chin pinched between her fingers. She's barely paying attention anyway. "Right. Where'd he go?"

I point to the far tarp flowing loose in the wind. My eyes catch on the debris below and my breath seizes. No—my breath evaporates. *Disintegrates.* The entire idea of things like *breath* and *lungs* and *oxygen* unspool because nothing exists in this new space-time continuum except the empty spot in the rubble where Mom's and Grandma's bodies once were.

The Hunter has taken them.

16

ONE HOUR UNTIL MIDNIGHT

"Will you chill out? You're making me jumpy," Aunt Jodie says as she lights her seventh cigarette and pops it between her teeth. She sits on the other side of one of the town square picnic tables, thumbs whirling through Fatima's monster book, looking for anything that might help us.

I rub my neck, cricked from looking over my shoulder so much. I don't care what Aunt Jodie says—behind every giggling table of teens or cranky sugar-crashed toddler, a monster lurks in the shadows. My heart thunders every time a black-clad Darth Vader or Harry Potter runs by.

Wind swoops over our table, sending a lungful of Aunt Jodie's smoke into my mouth. Fatima coughs politely, but I bat the air clean with a scowl. "Ugh, that will kill you, you know."

Aunt Jodie glares, then pushes a greasy carton across the table. "Eat your fries."

"I'm not hungry."

"You need your strength."

"No."

"Eat the fries."

"Fine, *Mom*," I say, and pluck one free, glee twisting inside at Aunt Jodie's disgusted face.

Ah, potato cut and sprinkled with sea salt. These once would have been a delicacy, but my stomach is far too knotty to eat anything. And when Aunt Jodie goes back to her reading, I slip the fry into Fatima's lap, where Rosie munches merrily on the end.

Of course I can't eat anything. That monster took Grandma and Mom, and I couldn't do a single thing to stop it. If I were stronger, if I somehow wasn't a dud witch with no mag—

Magic. The Hunter.

Family. Family. Family. Family.

The truth's sprouted in my brain, and no matter how much Roundup I spray, the weeds only grow thicker.

My hand slips into my pocket for the flower crown, wishing for some of Mom's confidence, some of Grandma's strength, but of course it isn't there. I steel myself, then glance at Aunt Jodie. "He's my dad, isn't he? Whoever the Hunter's using as a Host."

Fatima gasps and Aunt Jodie's hands freeze midturn. Her eyes flick to mine, and they're almost the exact shade of green Mom's are. "You touched him."

I nod. "I heard—well, I think I heard his ancestors. But you can only do Kindred with *your* family; you only hear *your* ancestors. When I magically pushed him back . . . I did father-daughter Kindred, didn't I?"

Aunt Jodie gives me an X-ray stare. Slowly, something melts in her gaze, softening her spikes and right angles. She sighs and, resigned, shuts the book.

"When me and your mom were in high school, she secretly dated Ridger Hern—one of the Descendants. It went south pretty fast. Ridger had a temper, and a concerned teacher called your grandma after a nasty shouting match at one of his baseball games. Anyway, she went ballistic. She forced them to break up and told Candice she was never to see him again. That he was getting close to her only to hurt her because of what she was. What we are." Aunt Jodie snorts, and some of her sharp edges return. "I thought they'd broken up, but a little while later she found out she was expecting you. After that she didn't have a choice but to leave."

Something buzzes in a far pocket of my mind, like an oven timer sounding in the kitchen but you're still on the john.

A mysterious baseball letterman jacket in a closet. The initials *C hearts R 4ever* scrawled across a diary. The way my skin tingled around Mathius, which I thought was just a side effect of hating him, but now see it was the tug of Kindred.

Stones roll in my stomach. All my life I wanted to know about my dad, and now I wish I didn't. And honestly, it's no wonder Mom wants to ditch me. Every time she looks at me, she probably thinks of her stupid, abusive ex's face.

But my mind whirls. Like all the ingredients in a recipe coming together, I finally understand.

"That's why you hate me, isn't it?" I ask. "I always thought it was because Mom had to leave town before I was born, because of the curse. I took her away from you. But on top of that, I'm literally half Descendant."

Aunt Jodie's mouth pops open, sending her cigarette plummeting into the grass. She quickly stamps out the spark. "I don't hate you, Adelaide. You're a Goode above anything else. And I don't blame you for how me and your mom feel about each other."

"Why, then?" I ask. "I mean, you seem to *really* hate her."

Aunt Jodie twitches for the pocket where she keeps her cigarettes, but she catches my eye and grudgingly laces her fingers on the table and sighs. "When we were little—like little-kid little, maybe five or six—we promised we wouldn't have kids until Mom passed, so we could always stay together. It seems stupid now, but I guess I took the pact more seriously than she did."

"You feel like she chose me over you."

The words flood from her lips. "I was her sister, her best friend. She shouldn't have put herself in a situation where—" She rubs her temple and takes a steady breath. "What I mean to say is, I don't hate your mom. And I don't blame you. I mean it. It just seemed dumb to get too close to a kid who's never here. And now—well—you're the only hope the town has left."

I stiffen. "The town?"

Aunt Jodie blanches like she's said too much. The way her face pales—lips first, then cheeks, as if the blood is actually being sucked from her face with a silly straw—reminds me so much of Mom. And the last time I saw her face like that.

We were at this very table, in fact, sitting in the same spot we are now, when Grandma had said, *If the fourth witch's soul is absorbed by the pendant—*

But Mom had cut her off. I thought it was because she didn't want me to get scared, but maybe they were hiding something. A fate worse than just my death.

My voice is barely a whisper. "What happens if the Hunter sucks out my soul?"

Jodie wrings her hands. "If your mom chose not to tell you—"

"Mom's not here. She's been kidnapped, and if I don't know what I'm up against, how can I defeat him?"

Slowly, Jodie nods. "In the story, the original hunters made one last stipulation for the curse—if the Hunter takes the soul of the fourth witch, not only will she die, but magic is erased from the entire town."

The glass in my bones turns ice cold. "But Sir George the corgi— his cancer . . . and Bogger's Bridge . . ."

"The cancer will return, the bridge will fall, and all the magic your grandma has done to keep this town afloat will disappear."

Fatima cuddles Rosie to her chest, eyes shiny.

"People could die," I say. A *corgi* could die.

"Yes, people could die."

A pit opens in my chest. This is bigger than not being abandoned, saving my family, or proving myself. This is about everyone. I swallow down my fear and grit my teeth. "We're gonna need a really good plan. Any ideas?"

Aunt Jodie slams the book shut. "Well, I can stew up all the ingredients, no problem, but the book says the spell can only be broken by the strongest magic. And you—well—I love ya, kid, but you're a little tapped out."

I deflate a little inside, but she's right. If only I could be powerful like Grandma or Mom, could tap into their power just the once . . .

Electricity snaps behind my eyes. I turn to Jodie, fingers numb with excitement. "Can I tap into magic on both sides at the same time?"

Aunt Jodie frowns. "What, you mean use Kindred with us and your—uh—the Hunter together?"

"Yes."

Her eyebrows rise. "I never thought about it. You would have double the connection to your ancestors though. It could be worth a shot."

"Ooh, Addie!" Fatima says, bouncing in her seat. "Didn't you tell me father-daughter Kindred was good for spell reversals?! What if—"

"I connect to both sides for extra strength, then use father-daughter Kindred to break the curse!"

My entire body buzzes. This *has* to be it.

Aunt Jodie looks hesitant. "I don't know, Addie. So much could go wrong. And anyway—how could we capture the Hunter in a way that you can touch him, but he can't take your soul?"

My excitement withers, but then Fatima squeals so loud Rosie leaps out of her lap and onto the table. "Addie, I think I have an idea! We are going to need my nana, a diversion, and approximately three thousand four hundred and fifty-two cranberries!"

17

THE HUNTER

In the bowels of the Hern Museum, the Hunter binds the witches. The ropes have been soaked in magic-suppressing hemlock oil— a trick passed down from Hern to Hern like their pudgy noses and flat feet.

The manor conducts a symphony only the Hunter hears. The walls hum. The windows rattle. The floors tremble, thirsting for blood.

It has been far too long since witches were imprisoned here.

"Where's my daughter?" the redheaded witch asks, writhing against her restraints.

The Hunter doubles her knots. She has all the features mortal woman usually do—two eyes, a nose, square teeth, and ten fingers—but nothing so attractive the Hunter could see as to tempt a Hern. They are *Herns*, after all, and this woman is an abomination.

Yet Kindred had poisoned the air when the girl touched them.

Unease sits like snake oil in his stomach. The Hunter didn't mean to pick a host who had spawned offspring with a witch. In his day, that would have meant the stake.

But time is running out. For he alone knows that if the fourth witch's soul isn't fed to the stone by midnight, the pendant will devour the closest soul available.

The Hunter palms the pendant. It rests on his chest, right over the entrance to the Dark Place. He might have felt a shred of remorse for the danger he put his Host in—for the soul caged in the Dark Place is sure to be the stone's victim—but the Host is not the Hern he had thought.

And the Hunter doesn't believe in remorse.

He reaches down to the Dark Place, tasting confusion, shock, and something coppery like guilt.

Good. Let him grovel over his sins.

"I've failed her," the witch sobs. "I failed her."

The older witch scoots as close as her binds allow. "Candice, look at me. *Look at me.* You haven't failed her. Adelaide's been blessed with a strong, devoted mother who's done her very best." Here, the older witch glances away. "Much better than what you've had."

The younger witch opens her mouth to argue, but her mother cuts her off. "There's nothing else to say, Candice. You were right. You needed a mom, and I was so busy making sure you and Addie had money that I forgot being a parent is more than just covering your basic needs. I wasn't there for you when I should have been, and I forever will be sorry for that. But—if you'll have me—I'd like to be there from here on out." The old witch's glare heats the Hunter's skin. "Until the end."

The redheaded witch chokes out a sob and reaches for the old woman, but the ropes hold her tight. Resigned, she collapses back against the slimy wall and nods with wet cheeks.

The Hunter gags at the display. *Foul, loathsome, weak—*

The Host lurches inside him. He swells with the rosy scent of *want*. He aches for the tenderness in the mother's eyes, yearns for the touch of the daughter's hand. The desire for a family who show love and respect courses through their shared body like a tornado. All his life he's been told witches ruin families, but maybe—just maybe—that isn't true.

The Hunter recoils, and as he does, something occurs to him. Something that molds his bones to ice.

Had he been misinterpreting his Host's emotions? What if it wasn't hate and disgust for the *witches* his Host felt, but for *himself*? Because his body was being used to hunt the hags.

As if in answer, the Host once more swims to the surface.

The Hunter crumples to the Dark Place with a scream. His black heart can't understand the Host's emotions, but he does understand betrayal. And that, he can't allow.

The two war for control of their body, writhing, twisting, and jerking like a marionette cut from half its strings. The witches stare in confused horror, pressing tight to the lime-coated walls.

The Host collapses to the ground, taking out a wobbly end table. Its drawer flops to the side like a dog's tongue, spilling old tickets, loose buttons, spare change, and a single, rusting pocket knife.

Gasping for air, the Host glances up. The knife's gleam catches his eye.

The Host's intent swims through the Hunter. *"No!"*

With a mighty lurch, the Host skids the knife across the floor. It thumps against the redheaded witch's shoe. For a moment, her eyes dart from the cloaked figure to the knife in disbelief, then she slides the knife up to her hands and saws at her ropes. Brushing her binds aside, she fumbles for the old witch's knots.

The Hunter claws, scratches, and bites the walls of the Dark Place, not caring about the pain ricocheting through his Host's body. He is fury. He is darkness. No one defies him and gets away with it.

"Come on!" the redheaded witch says to the older, hauling her to her feet. They rush for the door, but at the threshold, the redheaded witch stops and turns, watching the cloaked figure writhe on the floor.

The old witch reappears. "Candice! What are you—"

"He helped us," the redheaded witch whispers. "He . . . he helped us!"

A howl tears through the room as the Hunter lurches up the Host with the force of a thousand bloodthirsty bats. His Host's back arches unnaturally, and foam drips from his mouth. Inky shadows burst from every corner of the basement. With an anger so pure, so undiluted, the Hunter rips to the surface of their body, casting the Host into the Dark Place.

"Come on!" the older witch screams, and tugs her daughter toward the steps.

This time, she follows.

18

THIRTY MINUTES UNTIL MIDNIGHT

Here are the three reasons I'm feeling a little spicy:

1. I'm wearing a tutu.

2. Five gallons of hairspray may have permanently cemented my curls into the shape of a traffic cone.

3. I'll still be scraping glitter off my cheeks—I'll let you imagine which pair—until Easter.

Glancing down at the shiny CONTESTANT NUMBER 22! badge speared to the front of my costume, I swallow a sudden dryness and repeat the words again in my head.

I'm at the Miss Preteen Scary Cranberry Pageant. I'm actually doing it.

This is all part of our master Take-Down-the-Evil-Overlord plan, of course. But that doesn't stop the tights from itching or my pulse from racing. My fingers won't stop tapping a silly rhythm on the table in my dressing tent.

It's not every day you have to take down a supervillain. Especially one that's your dad. Especially especially in a tutu.

Muffled sounds blur from outside the canvas—the cheers of the audience, the drone of the announcer, the swish of fabric as pageant hopefuls rush around. It's enough to push anyone who's already on edge—well—over it.

Fatima grabs my fingers. "Stop moving. You're ruining my blend."

"Sorry."

Her brush finds my eyelid again. Her collection of makeup sprawls across the table in fancy bottles with labels I don't know how to pronounce. She tries to explain each beautifying step, throwing out terms like *blend*, *bake*, and *beat* like my face is a stubborn piece of pastry dough. She seems to know what she's doing though, so I don't complain. She's nearly concealed all my bone-glow.

"I can't believe you won't let me see your costume," I say, gesturing to the lumpy purple robe covering her outfit.

"It's a surprise. But don't worry, you'll love it! Nana worked so hard on the last-minute alterations."

Blissfully ignorant of Kindred, hunters, and Fatima's nighttime wanderings, Hakeem was thrilled when Aunt Jodie and I showed up on his doorstep to help Fatima—who snuck back in through a window once Aunt Jodie dispelled the Bubble Charm—design some last-minute alterations. While he toiled away in his workshop, Aunt Jodie raided Fatima's closet for spare fabric and set to work on turning me into something worthy of a crown. She cut, stitched, hemmed, and bedazzled with such determined ferocity that she hadn't lit a single cigarette since town square.

She's hidden from view by smoke now, but not the bad kind. Through the hazy steam of our potion ingredients, I can just make out her wild hair frizzing more with each stir of the cauldron.

Rosie, who had disappeared for half an hour—no doubt scouring the festival grounds for crumbs—now sits at the cauldron base tucking into her twelfth leaf of mustard greens. Her bulging belly sways from side to side as she munches—a good sign since she's our last line of defense.

"Done," Fatima says, dabbing her cherry-berry balm over my lips. She steps back and squeals with delight. Aunt Jodie's head appears from behind the steam and nods approvingly. "You clean up pretty good, kid."

"Good? You look amazing! Twirl so I get the full effect!"

Fatima pulls me in front of the mirror, and I do as she says. In my reflection, a sliver of tummy peeps out beneath the hodge-podge candy wrapper top and above the periwinkle tutu with a hem of dangling lollipops. Accessories, according to Fatima, are the exclamation point of a woman's outfit. She flat out refused to allow me onstage without her quickly crafted licorice-strapped purse. Everything from my highest curl to my ballet flats has been dusted with gleaming crystal sugar.

Oh, and I *literally* have gum-drop buttons.

But as I study myself, I suddenly feel a squirming in my stomach that has nothing to do with the Hunter. I cross my hands over my midriff and sit.

Fatima's smile wavers. "What's wrong?"

"I don't think I can do it. I just—ugh. You wouldn't get it."

She plops down beside me. "Try me."

My bees flare, and suddenly my tone has a stinger. "I can't go out there in this! People like me don't *get* to wear these kinds of things. You don't get what it's like—people deciding your worth based on what they see."

Fatima stands, shoulders taut and cheeks red. With a finger, she stabs at the brown skin on her arm. "I wouldn't get it?" She tugs at her hijab. *"I wouldn't get it?* No, I get it, Addie. I get it a lot."

"Oh, no, Fatima. That's not what I mean. I—"

She glares at me, and I take a deep breath and start over. "I wasn't thinking when I said that. Sorry, Fatima. Of course you understand. I just don't know *how* to deal with it. I don't belong onstage. What if I'm just kidding myself?"

Fatima's face softens and she scoots back down beside me. "Oh, Addie. The world isn't ready for girls like us. For dark skin and curves." She bumps my hip and I break into a small smile. "But it changes a little each time we don't back down. We strut in our skin, proud and sassy, and if someone doesn't like it, we'll tell them to eat dirt. *You* have to decide you're worth something, then you are. Simple as that. So, what do you say? You ready to go on that stage and change the world?"

I don't know what magical force brought me and Fatima together, but I'm very happy it did. I wipe a tear from my cheek and nod.

Fatima pops up. "Good, because you're going to kill it! Literally and figuratively."

I hiccup a sloppy laugh. "Nice."

"But seriously, Addie, you look perfect!"

"Not quite," Aunt Jodie says, and my smile dampens as she turns and rummages in her ingredients basket. Withdrawing, she moves behind me and places something on my head. I glance in the mirror and my eyes go wide.

Mom's flower crown.

Not only have the broken ends been made whole, but Aunt Jodie even added candy peppermints over each flower bud to match my costume.

"Now it's perfect."

I reach up and run my finger over the soft petals, just to make sure it's real. My voice goes all croaky. "But how did you find it?"

"Rosie brought it to me. I think she snuck out to look for it while I was sewing your costume."

I squat and Rosie hops to me, chest thrown out like a golden retriever. I boop her nose with my finger.

"Thank you," I whisper.

She licks my thumb. Then, from somewhere beyond the tent,

a withered voice rings out. *"Please welcome to the stage our next contestant—number twenty-two—Adelaide Goode!"*

Pop Rocks erupt in my chest as Aunt Jodie's fingers tighten. "You ready?"

The first real smile I've seen from her glows off her face, like one of those sparklers they put in lava cakes at overpriced restaurants. My eyes mist as I swallow the walnut in my throat.

A list of all the things I care about, all the people I'm doing this for, whirls through my head, blender-style. Mom. Grandma. Aunt Jodie. Fatima. Sir George. Bogger's Bridge. Cranberry Hollow.

Me.

I stand and gather Fatima and Aunt Jodie into a hug. "I'm ready."

Aunt Jodie releases me and wipes her eyes, complaining loudly of the potion fumes. With a sniff, she pulls her walkie-talkie from her back pocket. "I'll ring you as soon as the potion ingredients are stewed, then you say the incantation, okay?"

I nod, and with a final "good luck," I head toward the stage stairs.

The walk takes on a dreamlike quality—noises muffled, my limbs numb. Fatima says something at the end of the curtain, but I don't hear it. My name is called for a second time, and I step out into the dazzling light.

The cheers and applause are muffled as if from underwater. For some reason my breath crystallizes in my chest, and I have to huff to push it out. I can do this. It's just like following a recipe. Step one—walk over the three Xs taped to the floor. Step two—do a twirl. Step three—smile, and for the love of all things sweet and holy, *don't trip*, Adelaide.

With stiff knees, I shuffle to the first X, plop a hand on my hip, and smile in the judges' direction. My eyes adjust and the dark crowd appears in pieces. The glint of glasses. The curve of devil horns. The flash of pearls.

"Yes, I've been announcing this pageant for a hundred and three years," a brittle voice says from the judge's microphone. The speaker, Mrs. Girt, is the oldest person in Cranberry Hollow at a hundred and sixteen. She refuses to die—according to Grandma—out of sheer meanness. Mrs. Girt cranes her neck for a better view, making her earlobes dangle like meaty raindrops. "She is practically glowing up there. I've never quite seen a costume this *big* a hit."

The crowd titters, and my stomach falls somewhere around my knees. I don't know if she intended the pun, but how could I *not* think so?

At that exact moment, in that way that only a fat girl's can, my eyes find Mathius Hern in the front row. He's with his same boy from before, laughing and pointing greasy fingers at me.

"He's coming for you! He knows you're here, piggy-witch!"

My fists clench, waiting for the surge of bees, the flutter of angry wings, but nothing comes. Fatima's voice rings through my ears.

You have to decide you're worth something, then you are.

Boys probably laughed at my mom too. But she still has a room full of awards. She chose to be worth something. Not to prove she was a powerful witch or so some fatphobic bullies would think she's pretty. For herself.

I picture her so hard her face materializes in the back of the crowd. Her wind-blown curls swirl like flames around frantic eyes. My brain even conjures the ugly way her lips curl from her teeth when she's winded, and I'm struck with an unexplainable urge to laugh. I forgot she did that.

Phantom-Mom stops when she sees me onstage, relief and pride breaking across her face like the morning sun. A single tear drips from her chin. She looks so *real*.

All of a sudden, those boys don't seem to matter anymore. Raising my chin, I strut to the next X and strike a pose, flipping a curl off my shoulder. The crowd cheers, I grin, and for a single moment I feel on top of the world.

That's when I see him.

Ridger moves like a shadow along the back row of seats with a group of Herns. Palms slick, I slide up the ball of cotton candy on my chest, elongating the hidden walkie-talkie antenna.

"Is it ready?" I breathe into the speaker, tight smile frozen on my face.

Static, then, "It needs about two more minutes. Sorry, Addie, just hang in there!"

"Roger that." I slam the antenna down.

On to phase two then.

From my fairy purse I pull out a handful of my bake-off submission extras. Well, almost. It kinda killed me, but the slight change in recipe was for the greater good, so I pushed the horrified Gordon Ramsay voice out of my head and did what had to be done.

Waving the macarons in the air, I leap, twirl, and prance to the edge of the stage, then toss the cookies into the crowd like the generous sugar fairy I am. I might have beaned one extra hard in

Mathius's direction, and it may or may not have plunked him in the forehead, knocking him out of his chair.

"Ah yes," says a voice I immediately recognize as Mrs. DeDiggle. She sits at the end of the judges' table holding a microphone in her claws. "I have it on good authority Adelaide Goode's bake-off submission sat very well with the judges! Looks like we will get to try for ourselves!"

The crowd cheers and dives for the sweets. There is a momentary silence as macarons are gobbled by greedy mouths. In the second row, I spot a munching Hakeem, whose pleasant expression gradually dissolves into something more sour. Forcing a swallow, he gives me an encouraging thumbs-up.

I almost feel guilty, but I've got bigger fish to fry. That fish being the fact that in all the twirls and leaps, I've lost sight of Ridger. I try to keep my smile plastered on as I frolic around the stage, eyes and ears peeled for a swirl of black, the whisper of a cloak. Waiting for—

"Blech!" someone yells.

"These cookies are gross!"

"Is that"—a man smacks his lips—"*vinegar*?"

A gargle of vinegar a day keeps evil spirits away! I cross my fingers, hoping Grandma's old saying is right. The air in the crowd wiggles with hot stink-breath, like heat above a candle flame. My nose wrinkles at the fumes.

Then a shadow swoops across the sky, cloaking the audience in black. Thunder rolls in my bones. I clutch my chest in pain, unable to scream a warning, unable to look away as the Hunter dives. As soon as he gets above the dancing vinegar vapors, he swerves off in a wild spiral.

Victory pounds in my chest, but I know this isn't over. He'll come back for me. I glance up at the clock tower. Two minutes until midnight.

"Just like her mother, this one. Thank you again, contestant number twenty-two, Adelaide Goode," Mrs. DeDiggle says, her tone somewhat less enthusiastic than before she had my macarons. The crowd claps politely, some still grimacing and drying their tongues outside their mouths.

I take a quick bow and run into Fatima's waiting arms.

"You did amazing! And the cookies worked! They definitely bought us a bit of time!" she squeals.

"I know! I can't believe it." I take her beautiful, goofy face between my fingers. "Thank you, Fatima. For everything."

"Please welcome our last contestant of the night—number twenty-three—Fatima Tahir!" Mrs. Girt announces.

With a determined grin, Fatima squeezes my shoulder. "Phase three commences. Now, hold this." She whips off her robe and throws it at me. I catch it just as she snaps on some kind of strange head apparatus, but before I get a good look, she's strutting onstage.

The polite applause peters out. Every other mouth in the audience drops open in shock, but mine curls in a grin.

Fatima's costume is a smorgasbord of every monster imaginable. There's the fur of a werewolf, the scales of a mermaid, the wrappings of a mummy. Wires and tubes run down her back, animating her flapping bat wings and the glowing unicorn horn strapped to her forehead. Yet the entire costume—every claw, scale, tail, and tooth—has been woven together with hot pink thread and covered in silver glitter. The costume is 50 percent grotesque, 50 percent Barbie doll, and 100 percent Fatima Tahir.

Slowly, shock recedes. Then the crowd erupts with cheers, the loudest yet. Hakeem is beside himself with pride, tears glistening on his cheeks. Fatima struts across the stage, roaring and hissing like some deranged alley cat. The crowd eats it up, and despite how truly weird she is, I've never been happier to call her my friend.

I have to rip my eyes away, reminding myself we're here to destroy the Hunter. As if on cue, a gust of wind rips over us, whipping my hair from its cone. The breeze is crisp and clean.

Fatima catches my eye from the stage and our smiles drop. Fear stokes my stomach. Not as much time as we had hoped.

With a whoosh, a cloaked figure dives from the sky and lands in a cloud of smoke.

Right beside Fatima.

The crowd oohs and claps, delighted by the performance.

I smash the page button. "Aunt Jodie . . ."

"Almost ready, Addie! Give it another minute."

"We don't have a minute!"

The clock tower shudders with the first chime of midnight. Face covered in shadow, the Hunter's shadowed head swivels straight to me. All my bones shift at once, and either from dark magic or fear, I'm paralyzed.

Emboldened by the strength of the monsters she's wearing,

Fatima steps between me and the Hunter, daring him to move.

Then many things happen very fast.

With a determined look, Fatima presses on a particularly large mermaid scale in the center of her chest, lowering her head like a charging bull. With a loud glug, red liquid sprays from the tip of her horn, coating the Hunter. The sweet, earthy smell of cranberry juice hangs in the air. Below, Hakeem hoots and punches the sky, overjoyed his invention worked.

Sensing her human's danger, Rosie dashes out from under the curtain like a mad guard dog, teeth reared and belly swaying. In a whirling tornado of white fuzz, Rosie circles his feet at a dizzying speed. Pellets of mustard green poops shoot out of her behind with the fury of a Gatling gun, trapping the Hunter in a circle of death.

My heart leaps as the clock tower booms again. Down below, an oblivious judge speaks. "Thank you, Miss Tahir, for that lovely performance! I've never seen such a production! Now, if we could have all contestants on the stage for the winner's ceremony."

Trapped, the hunter cowers in pain, smoke rising from his cloak. He lifts his head, and even though I can't see his eyes, they pierce through me. Hate and malice and all the other dark things in the world wriggle up between my feet like maggots. The world goes white as he lifts his hand to strike Fatima.

I smash the walkie-talkie to my ear. "Aunt Jodie!"

"Done!" she yells. There's a muffled whoosh and a gust of purple smoke curls from my tent. Magic tingles in the air—thick and heady. All potential energy ready to be tapped.

Ready for *me.*

I run for the Hunter. My bones scream as fissures sprout like spiderwebs across my legs. I blink tears from my eyes, grit my teeth, gasp, sob—but keep going. Confused and shocked, the Hunter watches as I plow into him. His pendant flares nauseatingly white-green in my face as I clamp my arms tight around his waist and chant.

"By life, by death, by love, I demand to unmake, this curse and its binding, now break, break, break!"

But something is off. Kindred, my sunshine power, feels overcast. Like a dark storm rolling over the sun.

The Hunter wraps his arms around me, and I'm trapped in place. Silent laughter hums in his chest and I know this is his doing. That he's the shadow blocking my light.

Green mist rises from my skin, dancing toward the stone. And

I can't stop it, can't call it back. Pain explodes in my skull as the Hunter speaks.

"Weak . . . unloved . . . unwanted . . . give me thy soul and it will all end . . ."

Each soul particle that leaves my flesh takes some of my strength with it. The cracks in my bones widen and my whole body tremors. I shake my head, tears streaming down my chin, all my hopes twinkling out like smothered stars.

Sensing my death, my brain conjures the image of my mother again. Something to ease me toward the light. Phantom-Mom trips up the stairs, chest heaving, terror brilliant on her face.

I try to blink Mom's fear away. That's not the last image I want of her. I want a happy memory—the look on Mom's face when I baked cream puffs for the first time and forgot to add sugar, or the Christmas Mom couldn't get tickets for *Hairspray*, so we popped in the DVD and acted the entire movie out ourselves.

But Scared-Mom is still there. And behind her is Grandma, face red and eyes livid.

That's when it hits me. They're really here. Somehow, they escaped. And just like that, understanding sparkles behind my eyes. Of course they came. They love me—have always loved me—because I've always been enough. And maybe it isn't about proving that I'm Goode enough. Maybe it's about *unproving* all the bad things I thought about myself, so I can be who I was meant to be in the first place.

It just took a three-hundred-year-old witch-hunter to show me.

The cherry pit in my heart explodes. Power rushes through my veins, light and sweet, and bright as a sunny day. With invisible fingers, I stretch for my family and latch hold. A warm thread connects each of us, the ancestors' whispers and magic whizzing up and down the line like tin-can telephones.

The Hunter's block is nothing now. A cobweb to be swatted away.

Aunt Jodie's thoughts glide through my mind, more urgent than the rest.

"*. . . find the Host . . . find the Host . . .*"

My magic slips into the Hunter, butter soft. He's all dark sludge and howling wind. Through all the thorns and mud and anger and hate in him, I spot a glimmer of light barely moving, like a butter-fly with broken wings. With greedy hands, I catch it.

The threads and whispers double, nearly knocking me off my feet. My whole family—both sides—past and present. *Here.* Their voices are a coat of sugar, and dove wings, and the softest, richest velvet. Some I'm more familiar with. The honeysuckle and chamomile of Grandma. The anise and midnight bloom of Aunt Jodie. The Very Berry Kiss and bonfire flame of Mom. But others are new.

And they all whisper of how I belong.

Determination burning through my bones, I say the spell one more time.

19

THE HUNTER

Biting, searing, blinding pain rolls through the Hunter like thunder. He writhes in the witch's embrace, suffocating from the sickly sweet rot of magic. He must reach the pendant, must kill the girl. The pendant grows hotter and heavier on his chest with each chime of the bell tower. For if it can't have the girl's soul, it will take another.

With every ounce of strength left, he clings to the body. Kindred jolts down his spine, through his legs, into the soles of his feet. It rattles through his entire body like a loose shingle in a storm. His hold slips, and with a gust of magic, the Hunter is blown back to the Dark Place.

His Host shoots to the surface, dizzy and whiplashed.

"Kill her!" the Hunter screams from within. *"Kill the witch or perish!"*

The witch.

The little girl's magic surges once more and the Host grits his teeth, bracing for the pain. But the feeling is . . . sweet. Soft. Like the kiss of warm rain or the touch of a moth wing. Not the white-hot lightning echoing through the Hunter's flesh.

And then there are voices. They swirl through his head like a summer lullaby. Voices of encouragement, of love, of familiarity.

Her ancestors.

The Host's heart throbs, wild in his chest. Their voices sing of love and acceptance, of redemption and forgiveness. But mostly, they sing of love for the little girl.

Not one person has ever loved him like this, and the little girl has thousands.

"No!" the Hunter shrieks, clawing at the Dark Place. He tries to climb out, but every ledge collapses, every handhold crumbles. *"Save me!"* the Hunter cries.

The Host does not listen. He fights the Hunter, contorting in pain, but he fights. He fights for freedom and love and forgiveness, but most of all he fights for the little witch. The one he does not know but desperately wants to.

As the last chime strikes, the pendant glows white-hot. With a throb, it pulls through the air, invisible fingers reaching for a soul. It finds one and latches on, tugging the fighting fragment into its depths and swallowing it whole.

Onstage, the pendant goes dull. The chain disintegrates and the stone plummets from the Host's neck. It shatters on the floor.

20

MIDNIGHT

The crowd roars in applause as I collapse to the stage. The spell shatters—literally and metaphorically—but more so literally, because my entire body crunches once I hit the ground. I quiver as I hug the wooden panels, breath gone, vision white, trying to remember how to make my heart beat.

Then, like aloe on a sunburn, a soothing rush of Kindred slides down my spine. It works slowly, sealing the cracks, reforming shards, and calcifying my skeleton back into marrow and sinew. Cracking open an eye, I flex my fingers in awe, watching the bones reshape under the green soul matter dissolving back into my skin.

"What a riveting performance!"

"I simply must have a necklace just like that!"

"I say, their pyrotechnic budget must be quite large!"

It's only as I rise to my elbows that a figure catches my eye. Motionless on the ground, arms peek out from under the black, tangled cloak, limp and pale. I scurry back, but pain sparks as something cuts into my palm. Hissing, I lift my hand. The Hunter's pendant sits on the ground, shattered and lifeless.

"Addie!"

My head flies up and suddenly everything is whipped meringue and summer fireflies.

Mom.

She sinks to the floor and throws her arms around me. I squeeze tight and breathe her in, my heart throbbing painfully in my chest. Soon Grandma and Aunt Jodie join us—Grandma crying and Aunt Jodie trying to pretend she's not. At their touch, Kindred flares and our ancestors whisper their approval.

"You did it," Mom says into my hair. "You broke the curse. I'm so, *so* proud of you."

My heart glows. I glance around at all the faces, now safe. Hakeem—wiping tears—Fatima, beaming under a still slightly oozing horn, and Rosie, lapping up the puddle of cranberry juice onstage. Even Mrs. Girt, whose gleeful face is angled to the sky as she exclaims, "Oh, I just love the Fourth of July!" is a welcome sight.

And then my eyes fall on the lump of cloak, moving ever so slightly. The Host struggles to his knees, hood draping his face. Every ounce of air freezes in my lungs.

Mom yanks me back, forming a shield between me and the figure. The word *father* gums in my mind like old taffy. Slowly, Grandma rises and strides forward, determination boiling in every step. With a quick snap, she rips back the Host's hood and moonlight catches his face.

My mouth falls open, eyes darting between the man and Mom, shock coursing through my body like lightning.

Because the Host is not Ridger.

21

THE HOST

The Host glances up to a quartet of witches. Their expressions range from shock, anger, and disbelief to confusion. But he doesn't care. The little girl is unhurt.

His little girl.

His eyes rise to the witch holding her, the one with the lovely red curls, curls he hasn't touched in nearly thirteen years.

"Roy?" she asks.

"Candice. Hi." His voice is so small, so unsure.

"Roy?" the old witch says.

"*Roy?*" the sister witch says.

"Roy!" a police officer says, running onstage. Ridger's face is red with anger. "What happened? Where's—" His gaze finds the shattered pendant, crushed under the child-witch's feet. The look he gives her would have made the girl cower before, but now she gets to her feet and glares up at him. Strong and tall, surrounded by her family.

"But I thought—I thought *you* were my dad!" She whirls to her mom. "Your diary said, '*C hearts R forever*' and you had a baseball letterman's jacket in your closet! Ridger played baseball in high school!"

The crowd gasps. Several moms in the front row start chewing their popcorn with earnest, eyes darting between Roy and Candice.

Candice places a hand on her daughter's shoulder. "Honey, I think we should talk about this in—"

"No," says Ridger, face growing splotchier by the second. "No, I'd like to talk about this right now. Candice, is this—is this—" He chokes, so disgusted he can't get the words out.

His contempt turns Candice's eyes flinty. "No."

The crowd gasps again. Even batty old Mrs. Girt stops her prattling, turning up the volume on her hearing aid as her eyes blink hugely behind her spectacles.

"No?" Ridger asks, face a thundercloud. "Then who?"

But no one pays him any mind. All eyes follow the little witch, who slowly approaches Roy. The child's thoughts are awhirl, remembering the *R* in her mother's diary. Noting the red-and-blue watch on his wrist—the Chicago Cubs baseball team emblem now clearly visible—studying the familiar way his nostrils bubble out on the sides like they have been bee stung.

Her fingers tingle from where they had met his just hours before, sparking Kindred.

"He is," she whispers.

The crowd falls deadly silent.

Glancing from her daughter to Roy, the old witch says, "Candice?"

Candice bites her lip, then sighs. "I met Roy at Ridger's house one day. It was, well"—she blushes and turns away from Roy—"special. He was kind and sweet. So different from the rest of the Herns. I didn't start seeing Roy until long after me and Ridger broke up." She blows out a deep breath through her nose. "Addie's his daughter."

The audience breaks into a storm of whispers. A man in the back wolf-whistles. Ridger glances at his cousins on the side of the stage, expression half relieved, half outraged. The old witch looks at her daughter, confused, while the sister witch smirks at Candice, smug.

Roy gazes at Candice the way an artist studies an oil painting, completely enraptured. He'd forgotten how sweet her voice was, how her eyebrows arched when she spoke. And still, he tears his eyes away from the woman he loves to look at the little witch. Addie.

She doesn't have his eyes, but there is some of him there. Maybe in the nose, or the slight angle she holds her arms, elbows in, to her sides.

He wants to explain, to apologize, to hold her. He wants to get to know her, to find out what kind of ice cream flavor's her favorite, to know if she's allergic to strawberries too. He wants to—

"Ah, looks like the results are in!" Mrs. Girt screeches. Everyone jumps. Mrs. Girt opens the thick yellow envelope—which takes a very long time because of her gnarled fingers—and pulls out a slip of paper.

"This year's Miss Preteen Scary Cranberry Crown goes to—My goodness!—Miss Fatima Tahir!"

22

TEN HOURS AFTER MIDNIGHT

Like magic, twinkling Christmas lights appear in place of plastic bats, skeletons, and streamers on November first. Aunt Jodie rolls her eyes and mutters around her root beer sucker about "consumerist culture," whatever that means. She's taken a new liking to hard candies since she decided to quit smoking this morning. Something about keeping her mouth busy.

The whole diner is abuzz with chatter about last night, even though most of the younger kids have sugar-crashed bags under their eyes. But all I can think about is breakfast. Not a moment too soon, the owner, Mrs. Ketch, a woman whose dark skin and knee-length locks are always speckled with stray flour, slides a plate of cranberry pancakes in front of me.

"My award-winning pancakes for an award-winning girl! My busboy tells me you won the bake-off?"

I grin and brush my hair off my shoulder, revealing the bright blue first-place ribbon pinned to my sweater.

"Well, bless your heart," Mrs. Ketch says with a one-arm hug. "You hurry up and turn sixteen, now, so I can put you behind my counter."

"Now, now, Whelma. She's already growing up fast enough," Grandma chides, winking at me.

I dig in, trying to hide my Cheshire Cat smile behind a curtain of hair. Turns out, cranberries aren't half bad.

Fatima and her nana sit with us, Fatima still in her sash and Cranberry Crown from last night. Hakeem's having an animated discussion with Grandma—who for the first time since I've known her hasn't taken one work call all morning—about the quality of local fertilizers.

I'm just about to take a sip of my hot cocoa—extra whipped cream and cinnamon sprinkles—when the door bells chime. All eyes at our table follow the sound, and suddenly, the air goes electric. Stomach knotting, I turn.

Roy stands in the doorway, lanky, blond, scruffy, and unsure of himself in the way he holds his arms a little too close to his body.

He came back to Grandma's last night after everything died down, throwing pebbles at Mom's window until she let him in. They talked until early into the morning, snacking on my left-over macarons while the rabbits circled the couch hungrily. She answered all his questions—where we had been, why she left—and most importantly, why she never told him about me. Naturally, me, Aunt Jodie, and Grandma eavesdropped on the entire conversation from the stairwell.

"Move over," Aunt Jodie growled in my ear. "I can't see a thing."

I nudged her with my elbow, and she hissed in pain.

"Shh," Grandma said, peering over at us both with a stern expression.

"I couldn't tell you," Mom said in the living room. "No one knew about us, and even if they did, what would your family say if they found out about Addie? What would they have *done* to her?"

Hurt melted off Roy's face and I knew he understood. He played with the macaron in his hands, turning it over and over as quiet settled in around them. Aunt Jodie fidgeted at my side. Mom looked anywhere but at him.

Then Roy turned to her, eyes ablaze. "Candice, I—"

But at that moment, a rabbit snatched the cookie from his hand and dove under the couch with its accomplices. They both jumped, and in the commotion his words were lost.

Our table is silent as he walks forward, eyes flicking to me and Mom for a second before landing on Grandma. She stands.

"Ms. Goode," he says, inclining his head. "I've just come to tell you the Herns won't bother your family anymore, and we all hope this can be a fresh start."

Grandma's brows lower in confusion, but it's Mom who speaks. "How did you get your cousins to agree to this?"

Roy's eyes shift around for onlookers, then he leans closer. There's an almost-smile on his face as he takes a hand from his pocket and holds it out. A small plume of black smoke rises from his fingertips. "When the pendant took the Hunter, it left me a crumb of his powers. If they ever bother any Goode again, they'll have *me* to deal with."

Grandma blinks rapidly. "I don't understand. You're a Hern. They're your family."

"Not really," Roy says, stuffing his hand back in his coat pocket.

It's only then I notice how sad his eyes are. "I've never truly been part of the family."

I'm out of my seat in an instant, dragging an empty chair up to the edge of our table. Because if anyone gets how he feels, it's me. Fidos of a feather Fido together—even if the Fido-ing was all in my head.

Either way, I look up at Roy, and *jeez*, we really do have the same nose. Poor guy. "Then you'll be part of *this* family."

A brilliant smile breaks across his face, almost as if he's never heard better words, and he settles in beside me. Mom gives me a knowing wink, and I can tell she's proud of me. She calls Mrs. Ketch over for another coffee. Grandma sits too, an odd expression on her face. Her gaze flicks to Roy's black coffee.

"First rule of the Goode family," she says, passing him the sugar bowl. To everyone's surprise, she smiles. "We always add two scoops."

Roy gives her a shy grin and shovels in a Goode amount.

Fatima's parents show up around Mrs. Ketch's third coffee run. Her dad's tall with a black beard, and her mother shares Fatima's heart-shaped lips. She has a little brother and sister too, who flap around the table like pigeons, only slowing to *ooh* and *ahh* at Fatima's crown. Introductions are made, hands are shaken, and, too excited to wait a moment longer, Hakeem whips out his phone to show Mr. and Mrs. Tahir pictures from last night.

I catch Fatima's eye as her parents bend over the screen. She bites her lip, and under the table, I give her hand an encouraging squeeze. Brow furrowed, her dad takes a pair of glasses from his pocket. Cleans them off. Squints at Monster-Fatima.

"Huh," he says after a pause. "This is the costume you won with?"

Fatima nods, nervous eyes flashing between her parents.

Her mother plants a kiss on her head, then takes her face between her hands. "I think it's perfect."

Mr. Tahir pats Fatima's shoulder, a grin twitching under his mustache. "Very . . . ah, original."

Fatima's face is pure sunlight. I give her a double thumbs-up as her mom leans down to hug her. As she does, something wiggles up the front of Fatima's jacket. Rosie's head pops out above the zipper.

Her mom jumps back. "Ech! What's that?"

"Her name's Rosie," Fatima says, smoothing her fluffy ears as

Rosie purrs. "She's one of the homeless bunnies me and Nana help take care of at the sanctuary. Can we adopt her? Please, Ammi?!"

"Oh, Fatima!"

"Pleeeeease?! As a gift for winning the pageant?!"

Her dad squints at Rosie, who gives him her toothiest smile. "I don't know, gudiya. Wouldn't you want a prettier one? The eyes are a bit creepy. Like a monster's."

Fatima cuddles Rosie closer to her chest, complete adoration glowing on her face. "My own little monster."

Her dad looks helplessly at his wife. She sighs. "All right, fine. But you are responsible for her!"

Me and Fatima whoop so loud both our mothers yell "Shh!" but our glee is contagious. Our parents laugh, Fatima's brother and sister resume their twittering, and Hakeem shows anyone who will look the pictures on his phone. "Yes, that's my granddaughter!"

Soon everyone in the restaurant's clapping and Fatima stands up on her chair to give a bow. She gestures to her nana, and he does the same. Emboldened, Hakeem plants a kiss on Grandma's hand; she goes pink but looks very pleased. Sparks fly off the table like mini fireworks.

"What was that?" Mrs. Tahir asks.

"Some faulty wiring, maybe?" Grandma says, half-heartedly looking under the table. But there's a twinkle in her eye and—I blink twice—a magical *glow* to her skin. I look from Mom to Aunt Jodie, whose lips are curving into a stunned smile.

Because they felt it too. Sunshine.

I lean over the table. "Was that—?"

"Kindred," Aunt Jodie says, breathing deep of the tendrils of magic in the air. "Soul-mate Kindred."

I giggle and glance at Mom, but she's busy blushing into her coffee cup, trying not to meet Roy's steady gaze.

With a snap of my fingers, my socks fold and land in a neat pile on the bottom of my overnight bag. I zip the duffel closed and float it to the door, satisfaction curling my lips. Everything's officially packed for my first weekend at Roy's.

I learned a lot about him over breakfast—he cuts his pancakes into little squares like I do, he broke his pinkie sledding in third grade, and he's allergic to strawberries, tomatoes, and birch pollen. He also lives on the other side of the Bogger's Bridge and works part-time at the local auto shop, part-time on a cranberry farm. It's reaping season, and he says I can help on the bog if I want. He'd even buy me my own pair of waders. I've been trying to hide how ridiculously happy that makes me.

His leftover powers are a little concerning though. Grandma isn't quite sure what it means. I'm hoping she'll give me and Roy lessons together since we are both just getting the hang of it. My powers have come in full force since the pageant. When I asked Grandma why, she explained that since Kindred relies on family bonds, a Goode witch must accept not only herself but her place in the family before she can truly unlock her magical abilities.

Of course there would be some moral lesson to all this.

"Come on, Adelaide!" Grandma shouts from downstairs. "Your mom's about to leave!"

"Coming!"

I run to the mirror above Mom's old dresser, quickly smoothing my hair and outfit. The dress is a form-fitting sweater dress, royal purple and paired with gray leggings and boots. A matching headband pulls wild hair out of my face. Of course, the whole ensemble was meticulously constructed by Fatima, who decided purple perfectly complements my brown eyes.

I would have never worn something like this before, but turning this way and that in front of the mirror, I feel good. Finally allowing myself to just *be* in my own skin.

Sometimes even a baker has to mix up old recipes.

I run down the stairs, the Kindred threads connecting me to my family thumping in my chest like a second heart. The magic flows so naturally now, it's almost harder to keep it *in* than push it *out*.

Just as I felt, Grandma is waiting for me on the porch, the usual bits of rabbit hay sticking out of her bun and the gray Flemish Giant, Pam, squirming under her arm. Aunt Jodie too—a blue raspberry sucker in her mouth this time.

The car trunk slams shut, making Legs quiver, and Mom walks back up the porch to collect me in a bone-crushing embrace. A cloud of Very Berry lipstick and Mom's fresh lily shampoo folds around me in its own kind of hug.

Since the curse was broken, I've gotten both good news and bad news. The good news is Mom said we could move back to Cranberry Hollow if I wanted to. I said yes.

The bad news is Mom still has to complete her three months in Washington.

"I'll miss you," I say.

"I'll miss you too. But hey—this is a great fresh start, right?" She pulls back, and her eyes glide from me to Aunt Jodie, expression shy. Almost apologetic. "A fresh start for all of us."

Aunt Jodie squints at Mom, lips puckered around the sucker stick. For a tense moment, they stand there, sizing each other up. Then Aunt Jodie rolls her eyes and opens her arms for a hug.

"My God, Candice, come here. You're so sentimental."

Mom laughs and squeezes her sister. Aunt Jodie's smile is sarcastic, but I don't miss the new softness that has sprung around her eyes. Without the scowl, she is almost as pretty as Mom.

Almost.

Grandma wipes a tear from her eye and takes Mom in a hug next. A disgruntled Pam kicks feebly, squashed between them.

An engine roars as a black pickup truck rolls up the drive. Roy.

Mom stiffens and checks her watch. "Time to go." She hugs me one more time, then clomps down the steps.

Roy kills the engine and swings out of the truck just as Mom opens her car door. In two strides, he's at her side, hands clamped over the top of the door window. Mom pales.

"When you coming back?" he asks.

"Uh—Thanksgiving."

Roy nods, some color flowing back into his knuckles. "You know, you left before you even broke up with me?"

Mom stares at him, nonplussed. "So?"

"So, technically, you're still my girlfriend. And if you're my girl-friend, I'm thinking I have a date for the Cranberry Thanksgiving Day parade."

Me and Aunt Jodie titter as Mom turns beet red and fiddles with her keys. Then she gets in the car, starts the engine, and pulls the door shut. Roy lets go, mouth open and brows tugged low. Our giggles die.

Just as hurt starts to color Roy's face, Mom rolls down the win-dow and grins. "Yeah, I guess you do."

Roy's smile is starlight.

The four of us wave as Mom pulls away. I hold my breath waiting for her line to go slack, for her to move far enough away that my magic can't follow. But it doesn't come. The connection stretches like taffy, long and flexible, spanning across miles and mountains and moments. A breeze whispers through my hair, carrying a snippet of the ancestors' song. I close my eyes and listen, letting the magic roost between my ribs.

As if it's always belonged there.

Acknowledgments

First, to the true beginning of this journey, Mamaw. You opened the world of reading for me, and through that, writing. None of this—*The Glass Witch*, who I've grown to be, and all the lives this story will touch—would have happened without you. You live on through every word I write.

To my best friend, Brian, who I somehow convinced to marry me. I'm sorry I couldn't get your name in 250-size font and gold embossed like you wanted, but trust me, you deserve it.

To Dad, who gifted me my courage, my sense of humor, and a healthy amount of stubbornness—you allowed my goofy love of the fantastical to flourish into *this*. I would not be where or who I am without you.

To Mom, who always went 110 percent during holidays,

especially Halloween. You are to thank for my love of witches and escapist reads. This book wouldn't be what it is without your influence.

To my brother, Andrew, who would have loved to have listened to the audiobook. I like to think from you is where I got my resilience.

To my coven—Abby, Fazila, and Melissa—I don't know what I did in a previous life to deserve not one sister witch, but three. Here's to finding one another in the next one too. Hopefully we are rich and disastrously attractive.

To my incredible critique partners, Jessica and Lainey—I truly believe the way we push one another to improve and grow together and, most importantly, our friendship are their own forms of Kindred. With 100 percent certainty, I can say Addie and I would not be here without your feedback, dedication, and love.

To all my beta, sensitivity, and early readers—you have my utmost gratitude for your time, services, and kind words.

To my agent, Samantha—you've been my A1 since day one. Thank you so much for seeing the potential in me and Addie and being the absolute best champion I could have ever dreamed of.

To my dynamite editor, Tiffany—you saw what so many others

passed over. You really just *got* the story, and that will forever mean so much to me. Thank you times a million.

To my talented cover artist, Vanessa Morales—it's everything I ever envisioned and more. You nailed the vibe, characters, and emotions so well. I'm in love.

To the entire team at Scholastic—thank you for your endless work and support, and for truly understanding this book so it could make its way into the hands of the readers who needed it.

To all school and library workers—I hope you know how much of an impact you make on the lives you touch. Thank you for choosing Addie to aid in your magic.

To my YouTube channel subscribers—it's been a uniquely indescribable experience getting to share my writing journey from conception to publication with you all. I'm so glad you stayed around for the ride (and what a wild one it has been!). Your support and kindness truly mean the world to me.

And to you, readers, who are the lungs that breathe life into stories. Don't forget you are magic.

About the Author

Lindsay lives in a tiny apartment in Ohio where there are too many books, just the right amount of pet hair, and never enough houseplants. Or peanut butter.

She has a bachelor's in psychology and enjoys creating videos for her YouTube channel, where she shares her publication journey and helps other writers along their own.

YouTube: Lindsay Puckett

Instagram: lindsayjmp

Twitter: puckett_lindsay